Kaishakunin

A NOVEL BY
SHANE MCINNIS

PROSE PRESS

PRO SE PRESS

KAISHAKUNIN
A Pro Se Productions Publication

Written by Shane McInnis
Editing by Erika Williams and Gordon Dymowski

Cover by Brittney McInnis
Book Design by Antonino Lo Iacono & Marzia Marina
New Pulp Logo Design by Sean E. Ali
New Pulp Seal Design by Cari Reese

www.prose-press.com

KAISHAKUNIN

Contents

Glossary of Japanese Terms

Ashigaru – (light foot) a foot soldier; in the 16th century, these soldiers adopted the use of firearms

Bakufu – (tent government) the term for the martial government headed by the shogun that superseded the imperial government upon the ascendency of Tokugawa Ieyasu

Bokuto – (wood sword) a carved wooden sword meant to mimic the weight and feel of a metal blade and used in practice or duels to lessen the damage caused to opponents

Bushido – (the way of the warrior) a code of conduct and honor followed by samurai

Daimyo – (large, private land) a feudal lord whose fief produced at least 10,000 kokus of rice. This position was mostly hereditary

Daisho – (big, little) the pair of swords worn by samurai consisting of the long-bladed katana and the medium-bladed wazikashi; typically, the pair would be decorated and fitted to match

Dokuganryu – (one-eyed dragon) nickname given to Date Masamune after he lost an eye yet retained his fighting spirit

Donjon – (tower of imperial defense) a large, multi-leveled keep designed as a final holdfast inside a castle

Fudai – (hereditary vassal) the group of lords that Tokugawa Ieyasu marked as loyal and trustworthy after his unification of Japan

Gongen-sama – posthumous title for Tokugawa Ieyasu. Derived from the term gongen meaning a supernatural being, or Buddha, that has taken human form to walk on the earth in order to save someone/thing

Hashi – (chopsticks) Japanese word for bamboo sticks used as eating utensils

Hatamoto – (under the banners) originally a samurai in sworn service to a higher lord. This hierarchy was later systematized by the Tokugawa Shogunate to mean a samurai in direct service to the Shogun

Honmaru – (main circle) the inner citadel of a castle complex

Hori-hori – (from hori = to dig) a semi-sharp gardening tool; sometimes called weeding knife

Kaishakunin – (person concerned with beheading) the second in the ritual of seppuku who performs the killing blow to the neck after the seppukinin cuts his stomach. Originally, this was a full beheading, but as ritual progressed in form, the head was left attached by a piece of skin at the front of the neck. A kaishakunin may be appointed by a lord or requested by the seppukinin. If asked to perform kaishaku, one could decline if he did not feel he had the skill or the heart to follow through. If asked a second time, one would be honor bound to perform the act and face no or very little shame if he performed poorly. Being chosen as a kaishakunin was a fairly ominous event, and a skilled kaishakunin gained no honor from a job well done. Swords used to perform kaishaku were typically retired from use.

Kake – (hanger) a sword rack typically designed to display a daisho set. Some include a third position for a matching dagger

Kanji – (Chinese character) a symbol denoting a letter, sound, or word used in Japanese and other Asian cultures' writing

Katana – (knife, saber) a single-edged, curved, blade typically 20" – 24" in length with a long handle to accommodate a two-handed grip

Kimono – (thing to wear) a one-piece garment that wraps around the body and synched with a belt, covering to the elbow on the arm and to the ankle on the leg.

Kirishitan – transliteration from Portuguese cristão into Japanese used to describe the followers, practices, and items of Christianity in Japan.

Kodama – (tree spirit) a spirit that resides in and protects a tree. The Kodama may haunt a person who harms the tree in which it lives

Koku – (stone) a unit of measure initially meant to represent the amount of rice it took to feed one person for one year

Kusakichi – (weed base) a gardening tool with a wide, flat head used for breaking soil or weeding

Mon – (emblem) a crest typically associated with a clan

Morizuna – (prosperous sand) a cone of sand placed either just inside or just outside a gate used to greet an important guest

Natto – (stored bean) a fermented, sticky, stringy soybean dish

Nihon – Japanese word from which the English 'Japan' is derived

Odachi – (greatsword) a single-edged, curved, blade typically 48" – 60" in length designed to be wielded from a mounted position. Odachi were unsuited for close combat due to their size

Oni – (demon) originally an invisible spirit of misfortune, later an ogre-like being capable of great evil. Some were virtually invincible

Sake – (rice wine) an alcoholic drink made by fermenting rice through a process similar to beer brewing

Samurai – (to serve by one's side) a highly trained member of the military caste that holds allegiance to his Clan and his Lord

Sankin-kotai – (alternate attendance) policy enacted under the Tokugawa Shogunate that required local lords to spend part of the year in the capital city of Edo, later adapted so that their families remained in Edo year-round essentially as political hostages

Sensei – (person born before) teacher; master

Seppuku – (stomach-cutting) Japanese ritual suicide, it could be chosen voluntarily by a samurai to atone for failure, to regain honor, in a battle to prevent capture, at the death of a lord to indicate sadness at the passing, or in protest of the actions of a lord. It might also be commanded by a lord as a punishment. Women and those of low status were forbidden to commit seppuku

Shogun – (military commander) supreme military officers that effectively ruled Japan from the 12th to the 19th centuries; one who holds the office of the Shogunate

Shudo – (shortened from wakashudo – the way of the young person) practice where an older adult male would instruct a younger adolescent male in etiquette. The arrangement frequently progressed to one where the young male submitted sexually to the older, though such activity was expected to halt upon the boy's coming-of-age. Continuation of the sexual aspect of the relationship afterward was highly irregular and frowned upon

Tanegashima – (island of variety) originally the island in southern Japan where Dutch matchlock muskets were first traded to the Japanese, later the name came to apply to all muskets used in warfare

Torii – (bird abode) a ceremonial gateway that marks the entrance to a Shinto shrine typically made of two posts and usually two cross beams to form a doorway. These range from simple painted wood to ornately decorated four post pavilions with full roofs.

Tozama – (outside) the group of lords that Tokugawa Ieyasu marked as opponents or untrustworthy after his unification of Japan

Wakadoshiyori – (junior elders) high-level officials within the shogun's government responsible for many duties including information gathering and inspection of daimyo to assure loyalty to the Shogunate

Wakizashi – (side inserted sword) a single-edged, curved, blade typically 12" – 24" in length used in close combat or to commit seppuku

Yojimbo – (bodyguard) a personal bodyguard or security officer; sell-sword

Prologue

"Men of high position, low position, deep wisdom, and artfulness all feel that they are the ones who are working righteously, but when it comes to the point of throwing away one's life for his lord, all get weak in the knees. This is rather disgraceful. The fact that a useless person often becomes a matchless warrior at such times is because he has already given up his life and has become one with his lord." – Yamamoto Tsunetomo

The worst part of Kai's predicament was not the cage, or the bindings on his wrists and ankles, or the beating he had received, though all of those pressed on his mind. The men had also taken his katana, and he felt incomplete without its weight at his hip. As the guards shoved him unceremoniously into the cart, his hands went instinctively to move the scabbard out of the way of his leg only to find it missing. The guards had confiscated it upon the event of his arrest two days prior, and handing the blade over into the keeping of another was comparable to allowing another to handle part of his soul. His katana was more than just a weapon; it was an extension of his will and purpose. To Kai, it was just as alive as he was himself. Yet even the discomfort of surrendering his katana, and all of the emotions that filled the void of its absence, paled in comparison to the shame that he felt.

His father, Kikkawa Hidoyoshi, sat beside him, and his two brothers, Hidozumi and Hidosuke sat opposite him in the cage. Kai would have gladly traded everything he had at that moment, reserving not even his life, to remove the penalty that had fallen upon them. He refused to submit to the voice in his head that reminded him of his origin and the relative worthlessness of his life. He could not claim to share blood with the three men sharing his cage, but he would never allow himself to think of them as anything other than family. They had never treated him any differently than their own, and Kai had grown to believe that there truly was no difference. The three men who had arrested them did not share in that opinion, which led to the current circumstances.

His mind was free to wander as the mule-drawn cart trundled along the rough mountain path towards certain punishment. The bright green of the wooded mountains did not bring him any cheer. A jumble of memories and sequences flashed back and forth in his head. He had been trying to understand exactly what he had done that was so wrong, but he had arrived at no clear understanding. Somewhere in his mind, his father's words bubbled up from among the pool of memories, "One must always order the mind before he can order the body." With that admonishment held firmly in his consciousness, Kai closed his eyes and began retracing the events of his life from the beginning.

Chapter 1

"To find a retainer with a loyal heart, one need look no further than the house of a warrior who is faithful to his parents. A warrior should remain committed to his parents from the depths of his soul, or else after they have passed away, he will be filled with regret for what he should have done." —Yamamoto Tsunetomo

Of his real father, Kai knew only two things: he was a peasant soldier, and he died in the great Battle at Sekigahara. The hundreds of years of civil war that had ruined so many lives of the people of Nihon began its final chapter on that October day thirty-two years ago. The islands had endured the rise and fall of petty kingdoms innumerable before the arrival of Oda Nobunaga. He began the bloody work of reunification, but he did not complete the task. It passed first to Toyotomi Hidoyoshi and then to Tokugawa Ieyasu. Ieyasu's forces were victorious at Sekigahara, and a few years later he was officially recognized as Shogun, the head of the military state which ruled Nihon.

All of this history, Kai learned from his adopted father who saved his life on the day after the battle. The leader of the Mori Clan, to whom the Kikkawa Clan was a sworn retainer, had called Hidoyoshi to perform military duty. Hidoyoshi had marched to battle with the Mori Clan in opposition to the forces of the Tokugawa Clan. The Mori were strong supporters of the imperial line and wished to restore it to its rightful place atop of the political spectrum. However, upon arriving at the field of battle and viewing the vast armies of Tokugawa, several of the Mori Clan generals decided that caution was a better option. Coming to blows with a force of nearly 89,000 men was overwhelming. So while some of the Mori Clan fought, and died, Hidoyoshi, the Kikkawa Clan, and his Mori lord did not. In that action, they hoped to win favor with the Tokugawa. Such was not the case.

The battle was brutal, larger than any before or since. Tens of thousands of men died in the melee. Ieyasu's forces won an overwhelming victory thanks to his expert leadership and unwavering determination. The next day, Hidoyoshi began his long walk home accompanied by the small group of six samurai sworn into his service. As he passed over the field of battle, the wounded of the day before lay strewn about, covering the field like rice grains spilled from a sack. Many of the lower classes cried out in pain for someone to save them. Almost all the samurai left on the field had managed to properly end their lives with whatever instrument they could find. Some had fallen on their own swords. Others had found pikes or broken shafts of spears. There were some who were mortally wounded but had not been able to dispatch themselves. Like true samurai, they suffered in silence. Hidoyoshi found pity for those he encountered and lent out his dagger to foe and ally alike. It was a mercy to allow them to die with honor. Many headless bodies of fallen samurai gave quiet testimony to the destruction wrought by the battle. And on the very edge of the gore, Hidoyoshi encountered Kai for the first time.

There in a ditch made muddy with the blood of the fallen, Kai's mother had given birth. Hidoyoshi had yielded this story to Kai only after much persuasion, and Kai could tell that it still pained his adopted father to recount the events, even in memory. Kai's mother, a peasant from a nearby village, had walked to the battlefield in the hopes of finding her husband who had been called to fight. She knew that her baby was coming soon, and she wished to at least show the infant the face of its father if the worst had happened. Yet the child had come, and she had taken shelter in the ditch to rest. Upon arriving at the sound of a crying child, Hidoyoshi had spoken with her only a few minutes before she passed away. She had lost much of her strength and much blood as well.

Hidoyoshi's wife had passed away similarly upon the birth of his youngest son Hidosuke just the year before, and the sight of such an honorable woman, just as devoted to her husband as Hidoyoshi's had been to him, moved his heart. So then in a great and virtuous act, he picked up the mewling infant. Using his own banner, he had wiped the crimson off the child, and in the presence of his retainers, he vowed to take the boy into his protection. Had Kai been older and shown promise, Hidoyoshi may have formally adopted him, but Kai had never felt like anything other than his son.

Before the small band of samurai was able to get far down the road, messengers on horseback overtook them. Hidoyoshi was amongst the least of the Kikkawa Clan, which itself was not the greatest of the hatamoto banner-men of the Mori Clan, so it greatly surprised him when the riders delivered their message. He was summoned to appear before Tokugawa Ieyasu. At that time, Ieyasu made a great reckoning of clans. He named those loyal to him Fudai, and Ieyasu increased their domains and influence. The clans that had stood against him, he named Tozama, the outside lords, and he diminished them. The Mori Clan felt a special weight of punishment, as Ieyasu reckoned the Mori among the topmost circles of Tozama opposition. The handful of Mori lords who had not come to battle at Sekigahara, Ieyasu accounted no differently than those that had fought. This made the hold-outs, and even those barely counted as noble like Kikkawa Hidoyoshi, doubly traitorous. To Ieyasu they were Tozama, and to the Mori leadership, they were mutinous oath breakers. They then felt two hammers fall. Ieyasu reduced the Kikkawa alongside the Mori, and the Mori lords, bristling at the perceived lack of honor, reduced them to virtual peasantry.

The Mori stripped Hidoyoshi's domain, which had once been large enough to support one hundred workers, down to a parcel that barely produced enough to support ten. The Mori then forced Hidoyoshi to move into the hills of the Suwo Province, an area not known much for its fertility. Kai had only understood recently how much impact that had on his own life. Hidoyoshi's family had come so low that the distance between their status and Kai was, to many outside lords, not very great. It was not long before Hidoyoshi released the six samurai under him from his service for them to search for new employment. Soon after, Hidoyoshi began a swordsmanship training school to make ends meet. Though he was at that time entering his fifties, he was still one of the finest swordsmen of the Mori Clan. At first, his lowly status kept him from garnering patronage, but eventually, his reputation and skill won over enough to feed his household.

Much of those hardest times were outside of Kai's memory. Hidoyoshi raised Kai as best he knew how, and though he could not give Kai his name, he did give him a home. Kai never doubted that Hidoyoshi would have adopted him if he were able. The Mori lord at the time, still fuming from the betrayal at Sekigahara, decreed that the

5

Kikkawa Clan could not increase in size, not even through adoption. Hidoyoshi had no desire to marry again, so he and his three sons made the best of what they had in their small home in the mountains. The days were long but happy.

Kai never felt a single ounce of shame from performing his chores. Even as a young boy, he understood the grace that Hidoyoshi afforded to him. His brothers grew and learned how to read, write, and shoot bows, while Kai learned how to clean, mend, and farm. He knew his place and worked diligently. He was usually able to eat with the family, though rarely on important days and never when visitors were present. Yet within his soul, he harbored a burning desire. He wished for a katana of his own. Kai fondly recalled his earliest memory of Hidoyoshi's katana. The perfection of the arm-length curved blade balanced almost delicately in the hand, its weight offset in the pommel. The cord-wrapped hilt assured a firm grip even if wet. Kai could still see Hidoyoshi moving through positions, swinging the katana with the ease of a master, returning it quietly to the black lacquered scabbard at his hip until the handguard clicked into place. Kai was immediately and hopelessly enthralled.

His status was so low that he did not, at that time, even have the right to wear a single sword, much less the daisho, the matching pair of blades, worn by samurai. He understood and accepted that, and he never truly believed that he would gain one. Hidoyoshi had explained all of this to him. There was no room to question it.

So, for many years Kai watched the sons of samurai ride up the lane that led to Hidoyoshi's school to be trained. They were always so bright-faced and proud. At their left sides, they wore their katana openly, signifying that they had come of age. Most of them never acknowledged Kai's presence. Why should they? The few that did typically sneered or turned up their noses at the peasant boy in second-hand clothing, so dull that their color could not always be determined. His brothers, though, would spend the afternoons playing or fishing in the stream that ran down the side of the mountain. None ever caught anything, but they were together. And they were happy. Hidozumi eventually came less and less to play being several years older than Hidosuke and Kai. Once he came of age and began at his father's school, he forsook playing altogether. He was to be a samurai, and there would be no more time for such foolishness.

6

Hidosuke and Kai accepted Hidozumi's adulthood as unavoidable, and they enjoyed mimicking his newly discovered stern countenance. It was only when Hidosuke's own coming of age neared that Kai began to feel uneasy. Their different backgrounds would only be amplified once that happened, and Kai worked in his mind each night to steel himself for the inevitable. He would do his duty to his father, he would never utter a single word of complaint. His hard work and dedication would bring honor to the man and family that had saved him from an otherwise ignominious death.

The first few months of solitude were more difficult than he expected. To be closer to his family, Kai requested the duty of cleaning out and ordering the arrangement of practice implements in Hidoyoshi's training hall. After consideration, his is father agreed. Hidoyoshi was at that point entering his seventh decade of life, and though his mind was still sharp, his body was giving way to time. In contrast, that opportunity brought new vigor to Kai who was allowed for the first time in his life exposure to the swords he admired so. He was never to handle them, or draw them from their scabbards, but even proximity to them was akin to a spiritual event for Kai. And it was not too long before Kai discovered a secret that he afterward kept hidden for a decade.

One afternoon when Kai was a few days from his thirteenth birthday, he finished his household chores early and went up to the school before it let out. He thought to greet his brothers as they exited their training session for that afternoon, and he looked forward to seeing them. Upon arriving at the school, he found Hidoyoshi in the middle of a lesson. Kai knew better than to enter the room while students were learning. Instead, he crept around to the back. There he found a gap in the plank walls just wide enough for him to get a view inside. He scanned the room for his father and saw him only a few feet away with his back to the wall. Hidoyoshi always wore the Kikkawa mon on the back of his kimono when he was teaching. The crest was rather plain, a pure white circle with three, parallel, black reeds running in a horizontal stack, but Kai found elegance in the sparsity. Hidoyoshi was instructing some of the younger students on the differences and proper function of one- and two-handed grips on the hilt of a katana. As each boy held out his grip to Hidoyoshi, the teacher would judge the finger placement and give an assessment.

Kai was astounded at the simplicity, yet profundity, involved in the instruction on something as basic as a hand on a hilt. He felt compelled to try out the grip technique, so he took up the broom he had laid down upon discovering his secret peephole. He began to fashion his hands on the broom in as close of a modicum as he could to Hidoyoshi's instruction. Somehow, he understood the lesson instinctively. The grip was firm, but fluid. The fingers were not to clinch at the hilt but guide it. At that moment, Kai first grasped how to order his mind.

Each day thereafter, or as frequently as he could without arousing suspicion, Kai woke before the dawn and practiced. Then as soon as possible while still completing his chores to perfection, he would steal away to the school. He soon fashioned a bokuto out of a tree branch to properly simulate the curve of the katana and mimic its weight and feel when practicing. While he still dreamed of owning a sword of his own, the act of learning to wield one first was, to Kai, almost a rite of passage. Perhaps one day, far into the future, if he were able to hone his skills with a bokuto, he may be able to bring honor to his father in such amount that he could be fully adopted and gain the name Kikkawa. Then he could wear the family mon on his kimono. Yet some part of Kai understood these to be the fancies of a young mind, and each time he allowed himself to daydream he cut himself off soon after. He understood that he must not forget his station.

Everything changed soon after Kai turned twenty-two. The renown of the Kikkawa School of swordsmanship had spread to the ends of the Suwo Province. Challengers soon began to arrive, seeking to test themselves against the skill of the students of Hidoyoshi. Hidozumi and Hidosuke both participated in duels on what seemed to be a weekly basis. Under the firm guidance of Hidoyoshi, no student of his school was to agree to a duel to the death or even a duel using a real blade. While these rules irked some challengers who attempted to smear the Kikkawa name, Hidoyoshi stuck to his conviction. The family had been poor before, and he needed no outsider to tell him whether or not he had honor. He had endured scorn for decades since Sekigahara, and his old age had only tempered his determination. Yet when the second son of the Mori Clan arrived with his retainers and ordered the champion of the Kikkawa School to fight him to the death, Hidoyoshi had little recourse.

Hidozumi struck the Mori man down in three moves. The Mori retainers flew into a rage, saying that Hidozumi had provoked their lord into a duel. Furthermore, he had not allowed their lord to properly prepare himself on the field and thereby cheated by attacking too early. When none at the school and none of the villagers who had come to watch the duel supported this argument, the Mori became incensed. Hidoyoshi followed all of the proper forms and even offered the entirety of his holdings in payment to the Mori Clan for the death of its second son. The band of Mori nobles stormed off promising retribution.

That night, as Kai attended Hidoyoshi, a handful of the Mori attacked the house seeking Hidoyoshi's head. The old man who seemed such an easy target proved more than capable of dispatching two men in turn, but when the remaining three rushed him at once, Kai understood the need for action. Kai remembered that night vividly. His muscles had fallen into instinctual patterns. His broom was an extension of his arm, his soul. His opponent moved in slow motion, almost in past tense, as if Kai had been told ahead of time the precise angle and velocity in which each strike would arrive. He disarmed the first attacker in seconds and reflexes took over.

Picking up the fallen katana, he waded into the thick of the fight with Hidoyoshi. In just a few moments, the Mori lay in a heap at the feet of Kai and Hidoyoshi, all dead save the man Kai had fought using his broom. When Hidoyoshi looked at him in amazement, all Kai could do was drop the katana and flee to his room. That was the longest night of Kai's life to date. The exhilaration of using a katana mixed with his shame from spying on his father and concealing his training. He had felt more alive and more natural with the blade than with anything else he had ever done with his life, and he could not reconcile that feeling with the fact that he would never be able to do so again.

Kai had spent a very hard hour the next day as Hidoyoshi drilled him with many questions. Kai had thought that his father would surely expel him from his home, essentially dooming him to an uncertain death. Yet after the full tale was told, Hidoyoshi's heart was softened, and his anger cooled. He understood his own role in Kai's misbehavior. The discussion of fighting technique and proper form had frequently found a place even when the family was at rest or at a meal. Hidoyoshi had instructed his sons, even Kai, in the philosophy of Bushido, the way of the warrior. So then, he pardoned Kai for his spying. Furthermore, he offered to take Kai into formal service as a bodyguard.

Only slowly did Kai comprehend the meaning of Hidoyoshi's offer. He was first overwhelmed at his father's forgiveness and then by his love. But the offer to become a hired man brought with it an opportunity that was lost on Kai for a moment thereafter. Once the realization of the offer dawned full in his mind, he was utterly unable to keep his composure, and he prostrated himself before the old man. If Kai accepted the offer to be a Yojimbo, he must obviously be afforded the right to carry a katana.

The time between that moment and two days ago had been bliss for Kai. While he was still not permitted to attend Hidoyoshi's school, he did have the ability to practice with an actual katana. In those years, he gained such a deep understanding of the philosophy and mentality of sword fighting that Hidoyoshi likely had nothing left to teach him. He had everything that he could have ever expected given his beginning. Life was good.

Chapter 2

"Whether people be of high or low birth, rich or poor, old or young, enlightened or confused, they are all alike in that they will one day die." —Yamamoto Tsunetomo

A few years later, three men had ridden at full gallop through the gate of his home with a summons for his father. Tall bamboo poles tucked into the backs of their armor sported banners that were so black that they almost shined. The mon on the banners was embroidered in a lustrous gold thread in the form of three hollyhock leaves surrounded by a circle. It was the crest of the Tokugawa Clan, and though Kai had seen the mon before, never had he seen it so richly displayed. Kai felt certain that trouble rode along with the men. His prediction came true.

Despite his presentiments, the men and their gear continued to impress him at with every article he viewed. Kai had never seen anyone in such finely crafted armor before. Intricately woven cords held the plates of their shoulder and waist guards in a tight overlap. Light reflected off their polished leather chest pieces. They had been died a deep red and burnished to the point of appearing almost black. Even though one of the men began to speak, for Kai, the world stood still and muted as his mind tried to absorb their image piece by piece. Even the saddles the men rode in were obviously produced by master tradesmen. And they wore two swords on their left hips. These were men of rank.

Slowly, Kai realized that a conversation was going on between the leader of the troupe and his father. The headman had removed the black lacquered faceplate of his helmet to speak; it was frighteningly carved to resemble the face of a demonic oni. "Is the Shogun displeased with my service to him?" Kai heard Hidoyoshi asked plaintively. He had never been under any suspicion before, and whatever the messenger had said had taken Hidoyoshi completely at a loss.

"The Shogun has made mandate the sankin-kotai. All of you Tozama must spend four months of every other year in Edo. You will travel at your own expense, and you will leave in our care within three days," replied the messenger smugly. He crossed his arms over his chest, noticeably pleased with himself.

Hidoyoshi begged to be excused. He was well advanced in age, approaching his eightieth year, and the journey from Suwo Province to Edo was one of nearly a month. Spring had come very late that year, and as it was early in March, there was still the possibility that many of the passes through the mountains were blocked by snow. Even if he were to take a boat, out of Hagi perhaps, there was the very real danger of unpredictable storms and tides that were so common when sailing around the southern tip of Honshu at this time of the year.

Then in a final gesture of penitence, Hidoyoshi prostrated himself, his knobby knees bending only under force of will, in front of the messenger and spoke, "Forgive my ignorance, honorable sir, but I am still confused as to why I must observe the sankin-kotai. While it is true that my loyalty is to the Mori Clan, I have never harbored any ill will to the Tokugawa Clan. I have never raised my hand in anger against anyone loyal to the Shogun. I met and received greetings from Tokugawa Ieyasu himself, and Gongen-sama never required me to come to him in Edo ever after. Please cure my ignorance as to why his grandson now requires such an old man as me to attend him."

At this, the messenger simply laughed. His booted foot lashed out and struck Hidoyoshi squarely in the face. The old man collapsed into a heap, blood streaming from his nose. "It is not the intent of Tokugawa Iemitsu to have me explain his motives. His is the will and mine are the hands and feet that carry out the orders. Get yourself and your house in order. We ride to meet the Shogun the second sunrise from today. You will follow with us, even if it is in chains." With that, the man turned and remounted his horse. Before he and his two companions rode off in the direction of the village, Kai spoke up.

"My lords!" he shouted from a kneeling position. The head messenger checked his horse.

"One such as you should not presume to speak to me, and now you will answer for yourself or meet your doom," the rider spat.

***

The wheel of the cart hit a stone in the path, jarring Kai out of his daydream of the past and back into the present. He looked across the bed of the cart to where his adopted brothers Hidosuke and Hidozumi sat in bindings similar to his own. Hidoyoshi sat to his left leaning against a wooden plank bolted into the iron bars of the cage, the dried brown blood stain on his kimono clearly visible. The men had not even bothered to tie up Hidoyoshi. The old man's frail arms were bouncing along with the pits and stones in the road. Kai wondered if he was even conscious, and for a moment, he considered speaking to his father. He cut himself off, remembering the last time anyone in the cage had thought to say anything. Hidosuke had asked a guard for some water to give to Hidoyoshi. His face was still swollen from where a guard had grabbed his neck and jerked it into the bars of the cage in response.

Kai wondered how much farther their trip would last and how much longer their lives would last after they reached their destination. A breeze from the west moved through the valley bringing a chill to even the staunch Tokugawa men who rode on horseback behind the cage. The high passes were indeed still choked with the remains of winter, forcing the company to take the longer low road that skirted the base of the mountains. The cold had arrived late that year, but it had made up for it with intensity. The sun only peeked into the valleys for a few hours each day, and it had already found its way over the eastern peaks on its way back down. Kai shivered, but it was not from the cold. Each second brought them closer to Edo and the Shogun.

Perhaps an hour later, Kai noticed the sound of water moving along the right of the road. He had never been this far away from home, and he knew very little about the geography of this region of the island. The grade of the road pitched downward, and he was forced to lean towards the back of the cage to keep his weight off of Hidoyoshi. The sound of the water grew. As they continued downward, the bank of the road to the right fell away altogether leaving a drop of a fair distance. Over the drop, a waterfall poured itself into a frothy white pool some forty feet below. A shrine had been built at the edge of the pool, and Kai noticed several men wearing white loincloths, ritually bathing under the waterfall. The fact that men had deemed the location sacred did little to quiet his fears.

Between the road and the shrine was a clearing of some size. A well-tended lawn stretched itself out from the road to the shrine. A small but expertly crafted gateway stood about halfway down the path marking the gateway between the secular and the sacred space. Its posts and cross beams gleamed with bright red paint. Kai recalled a similar torii outside the small Shinto shrine up the hill from his home. Just inside the Torii was a station where water from the stream diverted into a pool for ritual cleansing of visitor's hands and mouths. In any other time, Kai would have enjoyed the scene for its simplicity. Today, however, it was horses, wagons, and what must have been one hundred armed men all flying the crest of the Tokugawa that dominated the view. A pit of dread opened in Kai's stomach. An armed group of this size surely had a commanding officer, and depending on how much trouble Kai had caused, that man may decide the fate of Kai and his family. He looked to his brothers. They had observed the group, and from the looks in their eyes, they had arrived at the same conclusion.

The failing light from the sun lost out to the chill of the western breeze. Kai began to sweat despite the drop in temperature. The three men on horseback rode past the caged wagon, obviously to notify whoever was in charge that prisoners were coming and that they required judgment. By the time the cart leveled off into the clearing and pulled up to the group, the armed men had started to bustle themselves into a formation. Horses were drawn off to one side and secured, wagons were pushed to the other side, and the men moved together to form precise ranks on either side of the path that led from the main road to the steps of the shrine. They stood stock-still, and for a brief moment, Kai marveled at their discipline. One of the three men responsible for their transport to the shrine emerged from the door and walked down the lane. He made a signal with his hand, and one of the soldiers moved to the cage door. The guards motioned for Kai and his two brothers to exit, and the bindings on their ankles were removed to allow them to walk. After they had left the cage, a soldier went in and hauled Hidoyoshi out like a sack. Another soldier stepped up to grab one of Hidoyoshi's arms. The two soldiers half carried half dragged Hidoyoshi towards the doors of the shrine which were still open, threatening to devour the Kikkawa family in one bite. A rough shove from behind made it clear to Kai that he was to follow. No words were spoken.

Kai's sense of dread was almost overwhelming. Each step he took seemed heavier than the last. He had never before been so afraid to walk through a door. It took a brief moment for his eyes to adjust to the relative dimness inside the shrine. Two figures were seated in front of him. The first was a young boy of twelve or thirteen years. He was not yet wearing a sword, indicating that he had not come of age. He was a very thin child, and as he tried to sit still on his cushion, he wavered slightly. Beside him sat a young man of middling height and broad shoulders. He had a small mustache and a thin patch of hair on his chin that had not fully come in. Surety and confidence radiated from him. Kai understood immediately that he was this man's subordinate even though at 32, Kai was clearly older than he. Both the child and the young man wore light blue kimonos. Kai had never seen any clothes so finely made. The shoulder folds were so crisp, Kai wondered if they were made of some kind of metal. Everything about these two projected wealth and power. Even the waist sashes the men wore were luxury items made of pure and radiant white silk.

One of the guards barked, "Kneel!" This was accompanied by a swift blow to the back of his legs that assured the order would be followed. In the tiny moment of free fall, reality caught up to Kai. The seated man was Tokugawa Iemitsu, the Shogun.

The man who had kicked Hidoyoshi approached Iemitsu, and at the appropriate distance kneeled. He looked to the Shogun who made a motion for him to proceed with his report.

"My lord, these I have brought before you today are the Mori hatamoto, Kikkawa Hidoyoshi, his two sons by birth, and one claiming to be his adopted son. We, your servants, delivered your sankin-kotai summons as commanded. The charged were given the appropriate time to make ready, though Hidoyoshi begged to be relieved due to age and infirmity. After delivering the summons, the one called Kai with no clan had the audacity to suggest that we take him instead of Hidoyoshi. As he had no obvious worth, I asked why his life was equal to a man of rank and status. At that point, he produced a katana and suggested that he was the equal of any man in a fight."

At that report, the Shogun's face betrayed his surprise and

interest. He shifted his gaze to Kai. Kai knew enough of the protocol to know that he should not meet the gaze of his superior, but something inside him refused to look away. The Shogun's eyes were piercing, and Kai understood that much was happening behind them. Those were the eyes of a cunning opponent. One capable of hiding feints within feints to disguise his real motive. Just as Kai felt that he was about to grasp something deeper from the Shogun's gaze, Iemitsu looked away. He motioned for his servant to continue the report. The messenger nodded and picked up the story.

"I thought the claim preposterous, as he was clearly not of any station worthy enough to wear a sword, much less employ one with skill. Yet his eyes burned with conviction, and I sensed that what he sought was to surrender his life as payment in earnest of his lord's loyalty. And being no samurai, he had no right to perform seppuku. Since I saw no threat in this action, and since Kikkawa Hidoyoshi was not one of the Mori suspected of being openly traitorous, I sent my brother Jubei, the least skillful of the three of us, to strike this peasant down. To the surprise of us all, he drew the katana and disarmed Jubei in one move. I then feared that what had been reported of the Mori was true and that they have indeed been training their peasants as an army to resist you. We restrained them all and met you here as soon as we were able. We have waited to question them until we were in your presence."

As the man spoke, Kai realized his folly. These men were not merely messengers, they were wakadoshiyori. The recently created body answered only and directly to the Shogun and carried his authority to speak and act. When he attempted to argue their summons against his father, he had effectively been arguing against the Shogun. When he disarmed the man to prove his own worth, he had struck a blow against the Shogun. His brothers and father had treated him as family so long that Kai had forgotten his place. It was illegal for anyone outside of samurai rank to train with the sword. Kai had proved his father a rebel when it was the farthest thing from the truth. Death was now unavoidable.

Iemitsu put his hand to his chin in consideration. He waited several ponderous moments before he spoke. "You have acted justly Hotta Masamori. Rouse, the old man. I will have his account before I decide his doom," he said in an even voice. Hotta rose and moved over to Hidoyoshi. The old man had woken up somewhere between the cart and being dumped unceremoniously on the floor of the shrine. The wakadoshiyori dragged him forward to the Shogun and deposited him several steps back from where Hotta had kneeled. "Explain yourself and your actions to me! How did this peasant learn to wield a blade?" he yelled at Hidoyoshi.

Hidoyoshi coughed a thin, ragged sound meant to clear his throat. He looked to Hotta and began feebly, "My lord, the boy is but an orphaned peasant. After the Great Battle, I was moved in pity to save his life since both his mother and father lay dead on that field. I took him on as a servant, as he reminded me of my own sons, deprived of their mother at such a young age."

"Spare us your sentiment!" shouted the wakadoshiyori. He moved as if to aim another kick at the old man, but Hidoyoshi held up is hands and shrank back.

"I apologize, my lord. I thought to give you the whole story. I will continue more quickly if it suits you," Hidoyoshi said hurriedly. The wakadoshiyori grunted approvingly, and Hidoyoshi continued. This time, he spoke more strongly and direct. He told of how Kai had spied on his lessons, how the boy had grown in skill, and the story of the fight with the broom handle. He ended with Kai being taken on as a bodyguard and with his tale finished, Hidoyoshi went quiet.

Hotta looked to Iemitsu. The captain had apparently never encountered something this strange before. The Shogun's youthful face was bent into what may have been half of a smirk. He beckoned Hotta over, and the wakadoshiyori obeyed quickly. The Shogun spoke in hushed words, indecipherable to Kai. A strange look crept over Hotta's face, but when the Shogun finished speaking, the captain did not hesitate. He walked over to his brother and spoke a few words. Jubei nodded and left the room in a hurry.

Hotta moved before Hidoyoshi and spoke, "You and your sons are charged with treason and are sentenced to death by decapitation." Kai's world collapsed. He had done this. It was his fault, and now his family would die a dog's death with no honor. He tried to speak, but Hotta held his hand up, sensing Kai's protest.

"However, the lord Iemitsu is gracious. If Kai can defeat the lord Iemitsu's brother in a duel, the three of you will be allowed to prove your loyalty to the Tokugawa Clan by committing seppuku at sunrise tomorrow," Hotta finished. Before the reality of the situation truly set in, Jubei returned. Tokugawa Tadanaga followed behind him. Unlike the Shogun and his nephew, Tadanaga wore a kimono that was an explosion of color. The base was a light green, but burnt orange leaves and light pink flowers spread out over the garment. He was a well-built man close to the same age as Kai, and Kai had heard more than one story about him. Tadanaga's feud with his brother was well known, as was his skill with a blade.

Jubei dragged Kai up to his feet and removed the bindings at his wrists. Kai noticed how much Jubei was enjoying this spectacle, and Kai immediately felt pity for the man. He was so clearly ruled by his emotions, not at all the way a samurai should act. Jubei shoved Kai over into the clear part of the floor and disappeared for a moment. He returned with Kai's weapon for the duel. It was not Kai's katana, though Kai longed to reclaim his weapon. Instead, it was a broom handle.

"This is ridiculous! I will not fight a peasant with a broom! I am a Tokugawa!" shouted Tadanaga. Hotta moved to him and spoke a single sentence. Tadanaga visibly tensed, and he moved to the open space in front of his brother. "It is good to see you, nephew," he said to the boy sitting on the cushion. Kai had almost forgotten the youth was in the room, looked at him. The boy nodded to his uncle and restrained a smile.

"Come, peasant, let me cut you down to prove how much I love my brother," Tadanaga said. Kai was unsure what to do, and it must have been plain on his face.

"If you do not duel, I will kill them dead where they sit. If you do not do your best, I will kill them dead where they sit. And if you lose, well, I think you know," Hotta growled, relishing the opportunity to dispatch the three men. The injustice of the situation burned inside Kai's belly. All his life he had heard Mori Clan members call the Tokugawa usurpers and challenge their legitimacy to rule. He had heard them curse Ieyasu, Hidetada, and Iemitsu by name in the village below his home, and he had never understood how those men could hate the ruling clan so much. But in that singular moment, he discovered that he too shared their hate. His family was as good as dead. Even if he did manage to win them the right to take their own lives and regain honor, he would still lose them. And for what reason? To satisfy paranoia? To provide the evening entertainment?

Jubei shoved the broom handle into Kai's chest with a grunt. Kai looked over to Hidoyoshi, hoping that his father might be able to offer any guidance, but Jubei thrust the stick at him again. It was more of a punch in the sternum, and it knocked Kai back a step. "Take it!" Jubei shouted. Reluctantly, Kai took the broom handle and tested its weight. He still could not believe that this was happening so quickly. He stole another glance at his father. The old man gave him a slow nod and took a deep breath as a sign to Kai. The quiet admonishment took effect. Kai could hear Hidoyoshi's voice telling him to order his mind.

Kai accepted the guidance and turned to face his opponent. He breathed deeply and slowly exhaled as he moved into position. He held the handle at the ready, just off of his left hip, with a two-handed grip. Tadanaga stood opposite him, his left hand on his sword's scabbard and his right on its hilt. The men stared at each other for a moment, then two, then three, playing out the duel in their minds. It was clear to Kai that Tadanaga would give him no quarter. The mood suddenly broke as Tadanaga looked to his brother, "Are you certain that this is necessary? This feels all too theatrical, even for me." Iemitsu's response was a razor-sharp gaze that might have stopped a charging boar in its tracks. Tadanaga shrugged his shoulders and turned back to Kai. The man fell immediately back into a state of absolute focus. Kai almost flinched at the sudden change. He was not given any more time to process the interruption, as Tadanaga attacked.

Tadanaga drew his blade and moved forward in an attempt to strike Kai in the same upward arc. Kai leaned to the left to avoid the strike while rotating his wrists down so that his weapon was almost parallel with the floor, its tip pointing away from his body. Tadanaga's sword swung past without hitting Kai, and the swordsman moved his left hand up towards his sword's hilt in order to return a two-handed slash from top right to bottom left. It never made it to the hilt. From his tucked position, Kai struck with a low-to-high thrust that ended with the tip of the handle crashing into Tadanaga's jaw just above his chin.

Tadanaga fell back, spitting out blood. Everyone in the room was amazed, Kai included. The entire duel that to him had played out over the course of at least a minute had actually lasted only seconds. The sound of clapping dispelled Kai's state of shock. Iemitsu had risen from his cushion and applauded the show. "I have seen many things in my twenty-six years, but to see my brother bested in a duel by an orphan with a stick has truly amused me more than them all. In the morning we will witness the seppuku of these three men, and we will ride for Edo after we have eaten," he spoke.

The Shogun's words set off an avalanche of feelings inside Kai. He felt like he was going to explode. The adrenaline from the fight ebbed leaving him cold and weak, or was that the assurance that his family was going to die? Was his lack of breath from exertion or shock? Nothing made sense! He looked to his brothers who both tried to remain stoic, ever the true samurai those. His father was as impassive as a statue and would not meet Kai's gaze. Tadanaga stared back at Kai, his hand rubbing the already growing bruise on his jaw. The whole scene made Kai sick to his stomach and as angry as he had ever been in his life.

It was only when Kai looked back to Iemitsu that his mind cleared. The Shogun half-smiled at Kai. It was the smile that a lying younger brother secretly gave to his sibling when the parents were tricked into punishing an innocent child. It was a smile of absolute victory with no possibility of recourse. And at that moment, the whirlwind of all of Kai's disparate emotions funneled down into only one: abject hatred. Iemitsu turned and began to leave. Everyone in the room except Tadanaga, Kai, and the Shogun's son kneeled. Kai had no intention to ever kneel to that man again, even if it cost him his life.

The Shogun and his retinue exited. Hotta came with Jubei and the other wakadoshiyori to retrieve Kai. Hotta smirked but did not speak. Jubei could not hide his chuckling. Kai, Hidoyoshi, Hidosuke, and Hidozumi were led outside to a tent. There were no furnishings, and there was barely enough room for all four of them inside. Kai heard Hotta bark orders to several soldiers, and a moment later four of the armed men took up posts, one at each corner of the tent. There would be no chance to escape. There was no way the captives could dispatch all four guards quietly and without weapons.

Kai still felt the burn of hate in his stomach. But when he looked to Hidoyoshi, he could tell his father was calm. The old man had accepted his fate. Sensing Kai's emotion, Hidoyoshi put a hand on Kai's forearm. "I have lived long, and we will die with honor. It is proper for a samurai," he said. Kai began to protest that he was not a samurai, but Hidoyoshi seemed to understand the argument before Kai had built any momentum. He slipped into the voice he used when instructing students and said, "We must live like we are already dead, and when our deaths come we must hope that they are good ones. Death is not controllable, the dying is." Kai heard the words, sensed their truth, but did not want to accept. "You three have brought me much honor, and I will depart this life proudly with that knowledge." Hidosuke and Hidozumi both nodded and each embraced Hidoyoshi in turn. Turning to Kai, Hidoyoshi added, "A samurai's life is not his own. It is the property of his lord. And as your sworn lord, I command you to act with both honor and wisdom. Many will say that there is no more Kikkawa Clan after tomorrow, but I say differently. I have never been able to give you my name, and that power has not come to me now, but as long as you live, my name will live with you. Do not throw it away in some brash display of fealty meant to salve your anger. If you truly wish to honor me, live." With what was almost certainly his final lesson finished, Hidoyoshi lay himself down and fell into a peaceful sleep. Kai did not sleep all that night. As the sky began to lighten in the east, his stomach began to churn.

Hotta arrived soon after with guards in tow. They took the men out to the waterfall where they were permitted to bathe. Then, they were moved to the clearing. A screen had been set up facing the east. In front of the screen, mats had been placed several deep. In the front of all, several chairs had been set facing the screen. Tokugawa Iemitsu, his son, and his brother sat in them. Around the three witnesses, retainers stood at attention.

A soldier led Hidoyoshi, Hidosuke, and Hidozumi to the mats where each kneeled quietly and with reverence. Another held Kai just to the left of the screen. Kai looked at the katana of the guard standing next to him. How easy would it have been for him to take the sword, dispatch the guards, and charge the Shogun? Yet, he made no move. No binds had been on the men all morning. Hotta and the guards expected nothing short of their full cooperation and had any of the condemned caused trouble he would have been struck down on the spot. Honor had secured their complacence. Honor was the binding that held them to task. Hotta rose to speak.

"To prove your loyalty to the Tokugawa Clan, you have chosen to commit seppuku. This is an honorable death, and your actions today will be remembered." As it was unaccustomed to speak overlong, or at all, at a seppuku ceremony, the Shogun nodded at

Hotta and sat back down. Kai felt a hand around his arm pulling him behind the screen. There, three trays of food had been prepared. Hotta pointed at them, and Kai understood only then what had been expected of him. He was to act as the kaishakunin.

"Oldest to young," was the only thing that the guard said. An uncontrollable swirl of emotions threatened to break Kai's composure. He knew the proper forms, and he knew that he had the skill to perform the task, but how? Why? He took one step towards the trays, but his knees gave way. Hotta's hand grabbed the back of his kimono, preventing Kai from falling. His other hand went to his sword, though he did not draw. Kai fought to steel himself against his own emotions, to regain a stoic demeanor. It was not befitting of a man to be conquered by his feelings, and he told himself that the lapse was due only to the surprise that came with the task now set before him. If he failed as kaishakunin, it would bring shame on himself and his family. This must not be so. He was already responsible for them being in this predicament, he would not rob them of their honor. Hidoyoshi's words from the night before replayed in his head. Honor and wisdom.

Kai walked over to the trays. They were sparsely set with a very meager meal and a small cup of sake. One by one he took them out to the mats in front of his brothers, then his father. The men ate and drank only what was expected. Not so much that it appeared they were delaying fate, but not so little as to appear weak stomached. Kai returned after the meal with the instruments of their doom. Each man's wakizashi blade had been removed from the hilt and wrapped with paper. Kai placed them at the top of each tray, just slightly out of normal reach. He returned to the tables and distributed writing utensils and parchment.

Each man took but a brief moment to record a poem. They had no doubt been at least partly prepared ahead of time. The silence of the ceremony was palpable. Since Hotta's brief instruction, not a word had been spoken. Even Kai's footfalls were muffled by the grass and mats. He was too far away to hear the strokes of the brushes on the parchment, but somehow he believed that they were absolutely inaudible. He understood that the most important phase of his task was rapidly approaching. All of the things that he wanted to say were building up inside him challenging his resolve. He wanted to shout curses at the Tokugawa. He wanted to tell his father and brothers that he loved them. He wanted to beg the gods for intervention. He wanted to sob wordless cries against the injustices of the world in which he lived. But he did none of those things. Instead, he went to collect everything from the trays except the blades.

As he deposited the items behind the screen, his guard produced Kai's own sword and handed it to the kaishakunin. Kai ground his teeth but accepted the blade. His role in today's events was ominous already. Even a perfect completion of his task would garner him no honor of his own. But to make him use his own sword was surely some kind of Tokugawa trick to add another element of discomfort. Swords used for the deathblow were considered somewhat tainted from the act. He walked quietly behind the kneeling men and stopped just to the left of Hidoyoshi. The old man understood, and removed his arms from his kimono, tucking his sleeves under his legs. It was permitted now for Kai to speak proscribed words, and despite the fact they were ultimately scripted, they took on a new meaning in the situation.

"Sir, I have been designated as your assistant. Rest assured, I shall not fail you," he said. Hidoyoshi made no sign that he heard what Kai has said, he had locked gazes with the Shogun. He reached out to the tray and pulled it slightly towards him so that he was able to reach the blade. His ancient and weathered hands, gnarled by arthritis, still knew how to properly grip the weapon as if the repetition of time had made the action as instinctual as breathing. He placed the tip of the blade on the left side of his stomach. His skin parted as thin paper when he pushed the blade in. With deliberate slowness and without once breaking eye contact with Iemitsu, Hidoyoshi dragged the blade in a line above his navel from left to right.

Kai had taken the proper stance behind his father, his sword held in his right-hand parallel to the ground. He felt glad that he was not able to see the full view of his father's cut. He felt almost certain that it would have thrown him from his own task. When his father's hands pushed the blade fully across his stomach to the right, Kai struck quickly. His sword came down in one smooth motion, aiming at a position just above where his father's neck met his right shoulder. His left hand met the hilt only just before the blade hit its target. Kai's skill with his katana made certain that the first blow finished the job, and his father's head fell with a light thump just in front of his body. Even in death, the old sword master's hands still gripped his weapon.

Kai turned slightly, making certain to not expose his back to the witnesses, and shook the blood from his blade. Kneeling behind his father's body, he used a prepared sheet of paper to wipe his blade before returning it to his scabbard. Then, grasping his father's head by the topknot, he held it aloft for the Tokugawa to approve, first in profile, then in front. He looked to his two brothers, then to the Shogun who wore that same half smile of self-satisfaction. Kai's task was far from over.

Chapter 3

"A warrior is worthless unless he rises above others and stands strong in the midst of a storm." — Yamamoto Tsunetomo

Hidozumi and Hidosuke followed their father into death in exactly the same manner. Kai performed the kaishaku, the deathblow, perfectly each time, and each time he was forced to end the life of one of his family members a part of who he was burned away. By the time he held Hidosuke's head aloft for inspection, Kai felt as if the ordeal had utterly consumed him. He stood before the witnesses to the seppuku as some sort of non-man, only a remnant of an actual person. What remained of his being was a smoldering bed of hatred for Iemitsu.

Hotta came out to the padding and reclaimed Kai's katana. The wakadoshiyori attempted to push Kai into a kneeling position, but Kai resisted. He would not kneel. Hotta struck him again in the back of the knees, but Kai's vow held his legs in place. "Never again in the presence of Iemitsu," he said quietly. Hotta stepped back, determined to break Kai's shin if need be, but Iemitsu rose and held up his hand. To the surprise of all of those in attendance, the Shogun made his way across the small open space between the seats and mats and stopped directly in front of Kai.

"You hate me don't you?" he asked Kai. This was surely a rhetorical question, as Kai had no right to speak directly to the Shogun unless given specific permission. Iemitsu looked the older man over. Kai tried to relax his hands which were balled into fists at his sides, but the Shogun noticed the attempt. "You truly wish me dead, and you would kill me yourself right now with your bare hands if you thought that you could accomplish the task before Hotta struck you down," he said in a tone that displayed as much amusement as it did contempt.

"I find you fascinating, I must confess. You have no family, yet you have so far conducted yourself with honor. You have no station, yet you perform the duties of a samurai to perfection. Now you have no lord, no duty, and no purpose. All that you had lies dead behind you, and you still show such spirit. So many of the people around me say only what they believe that I want to hear, and they only do what they believe I want them to do. To have someone such as yourself display an opinion of his own is honestly rather refreshing. You are a rarity that I wish to study further," Iemitsu declared. Kai heard little of what was said. His mind was filled with calculations and estimations. How close did Iemitsu need to walk for Kai to be able to strike? Would it be wiser to strike at the nose to drive it into the brain or did he have time to deliver several strikes to the temple? How long did he have before Hotta drew his sword and moved around the Shogun to get at Kai? Yet Hidoyoshi's words won out in the end. His father had known that Kai would accept death freely to gain his revenge against Iemitsu. Hidoyoshi proved his wisdom even from beyond this life. Despite his desire to wrap his hands around the shogun's throat and hold on for as long as it took, Kai fought to calm himself.

Iemitsu seemed to read Kai's thoughts and took a step backward, smiling as he did. "Do you not understand that today I extended an unwarranted grace to your family? I have done absolutely nothing that could be deemed dishonorable." He spread his hands out as if to offer himself to Kai for inspection. Kai simply stared at his own feet. He did not want to risk meeting Iemitsu's gaze. The man was clearly perceptive, and Kai feared giving himself away any more. Iemitsu chuckled. He seemed genuinely amused by Kai's reactions. No one in the crowd would have batted an eye if the Shogun had commanded Hotta to remove Kai's head at that very moment, and from the way, Hotta's jaw was grinding it was clear that he hoped such an order would come soon.

"Load him back into the cart. Give him food and water. He will come with us to Edo," Iemitsu said instead. Hotta's mouth gaped open in a vain search for words, and Iemitsu chuckled again upon seeing his general's look of bewilderment. Yet his word was law, and he did not repeat himself. Instead, he turned and walked back to his chair, making certain that none of the blood from the recently deceased stained his clothes, blameless and guilty all at once.

Jubei and the other wakadoshiyori came to Kai and grabbed him by the upper arms. They hauled him bodily across the clearing and dumped him back into the caged cart. Hotta came a few moments later with a tiny portion of rice and a cup of water that held two mouthfuls at best. He apparently expected Kai to eat with his hands, as he had not provided any hashi. Kai supposed that the man considered even a chopstick a possible weapon. "I do not understand what my lord has in store for you, but I give you my word and call all of my ancestors to attend this vow: If you so much as raise a finger against Tokugawa Iemitsu I will burn your body and scatter whatever is left to the far corners of Nihon."

Kai said nothing. He ate with his fingers, saving the few sips of water he had until the end. He watched as the retainers and soldiers ate a quick meal then began to break camp in preparation for their journey. Horses were brought from behind the shrine where they had apparently been stabled for the night. Just short of an hour later, the entire retinue moved out onto the northward path. No one had spoken with Kai since Hotta made his vow, and Kai expected little company. He used his time alone to begin his plot of revenge. He was unsure as to how long Iemitsu planned on sparing his life, but he doubted that the Shogun would continue to delay sentence based solely on amusement. Kai needed to make himself important somehow. For that, he needed information.

The group traveled well into the afternoon, halting only briefly at lunch. With every mile, the mountains to their sides dropped in height, and the path bent more and more to the east. Kai could only guess where the route they were traveling. His best reckoning was that they would head to Hiroshima on the eastern shore of Nihon and then turn north along the flatter and more open ground. But he did not know how long that would take. Weeks perhaps. And then what? A city the size of Edo was beyond Kai's ability to imagine.

By the time the group made camp, the moon had already appeared in the sky. It was almost full, and Kai could see much of the activity of the camp from its light. Soon cookfires added their smaller lights to the scene. A soldier came by with another serving of rice and water for Kai. The portion of both was significantly larger than what Hotta had delivered, and Kai wanted to believe that signified a more open mind. "How many days to Edo?" Kai asked the guard before he moved out of earshot. The man paused as if to answer, but after a moment of contemplation, he turned and walked away.

Kai wondered how deep the loyalty of the men ran. Could he ingratiate himself to any of them enough to produce an advantage? He doubted he would get more than one chance at Iemitsu. It needed to be foolproof.

The next two days passed in much the same way. Kai was fed but kept on the edge of starvation. In an attempt to cheer himself, he adopted the idea that everyone in the honor guard was terribly afraid of him at his full strength. It did not help much. Kai slowly grew more despondent. He had already run through a dozen times a dozen scenarios where he broke out of the cage, acquired a blade, and cut his way to the Shogun. Even with his skill, though, he knew that it was ridiculous to put any weight into the plans. He did it mostly to keep his mind busy. The only person that had spoken directly to him was a guard who gave Kai his name, Masutomo when Kai inquired. It surprised him all the more, then when the Shogun's brother and son rode up to his cage.

They had allowed the party to pass them as they made a detour down a small trail that ran off into the forest on the right. From his observations, Kai had learned that the son, Ienobu, was very interested in shrines and holy places. He inferred that the path must have led to just such a destination. Kai's wagon cage was far in the rear of the procession, so he was among the first to be overtaken as the two pilgrims made their way back to the head of the line. Kai had fully expected them to continue past without even so much as a glance, but he was wrong.

Tadanaga checked the trot of his horse to make pace with Kai's wagon. He left enough room for Ienobu to ride up between him and the wagon. His jaw was a sickly mot of yellow and purple in the place where Kai had struck him in their duel. "Greetings, fellow traveler!" Tadanaga said in a surprisingly friendly tone. Kai's face must have betrayed his feelings, as Tadanaga laughed. "I am not my brother, my worthy opponent. We share blood but not temperament. You may speak with either of us as you will," said Tadanaga including Ienobu in the conversation.

"What would you have me say, honorable lord?" Kai asked. Was this the opportunity for which he had been hoping?

"I would know if you possess the skill to teach as well as you wield," Ienobu said plainly. Kai's gaze fell in an appraisal of the prince. The boy was neither tall nor broad of shoulder. That would be to his disadvantage, as he would not be able to generate much power with his blade. Yet, Kai sensed that his size and stature would lend him quickness in compensation for a dearth of power. The blade did the cutting, not the muscles.

Despite the seeming honesty of the two lords, Kai still felt a sense of wariness. "What I learned from my father, I learned without being directly taught," he said in a measured and flat tone. It was a true and innocuous statement. He decided to allow them to dictate the pace of the conversation despite a large portion of his mind that craved escape and still clung to hope.

An understanding smile crossed the face of Tadanaga. "Kai, I give you my word in the presence of my ancestors, and I call the Kodama spirit of every tree in this forest as a witness that neither I nor my nephew pose you any threat or wish you any ill. Quite the opposite is true. You have acted honorably in an exceedingly difficult situation and displayed more skill in fighting than any I have ever faced. The Prince wishes to learn from you. I have taught him for several years when I have the chance, but I believe that I am being sent away from Edo soon after we arrive. My brother and I cannot help but disagree over…many things," Tadanaga spoke in a familiar tone.

Kai was quiet for a moment. He understood that he was in a duel. His life was definitely on the line. Iemitsu was his opponent, and once again it seemed that Kai had only a broomstick to defend himself. Tadanaga and Ienobu seemed to have legitimate and honest motives, but even so, a part of his mind wondered if this was part of an elaborate scheme from Iemitsu. No, he decided. If Iemitsu wished him dead, he would have been killed back at the waterfall shrine. The Shogun did not seem patient enough to plot. "I can teach if you can learn," he said solemnly and directly to Ienobu.

"Good!" boomed Tadanaga. Ienobu was more reserved, but there was an undoubtable smile on his face.

"Guard, stop the wagon and release this man," the Prince said to the wagon driver. To another, he said, "Go to the horses and bring one of the spares to us." The men set themselves to their tasks. Kai had a hard time believing how quickly his fate had changed. The guard driving the wagon had already opened the door to the cage and was gesturing for Kai to exit. It took a moment for reality to register in Kai's mind. "You are free to exit and ride with us," Ienobu spoke.

The words shook Kai from his stupor. He stood as much as was possible and shuffled to the back of the cage. Upon extricating himself, he stretched himself up to his full height.

"Lords, I have no right to do anything but thank you for your kindness and generosity. However, I do have one question on which I beg your indulgence," Kai asked with his head bowed reverently.

"My word," Tadanaga huffed, "will it take me formally adopting you as a son for you to understand that neither of us cares for formality?" Kai refused to allow the instant familiarity to force his mental guard down.

"I will take that as assent. How will the Shogun react to this?" Kai asked.

"Don't worry about him. I have already spoken about you being hired on in my place. He admitted to being rather intrigued by you. I should warn you that holding his interest is not as secure as it sounds. I believe that you are just his new toy. He seems to want to figure out how you work so that he can use you to his gains. And, much like a child with a toy, he is more than capable of breaking you if he finds you unsuitable. All that dreariness aside though, a young man should know how to wield a blade. Since Iemitsu spent more time bathing his instructor than learning technique, he is absolutely useless in a fight," Tadanaga said. Then to himself, he added, "Oh, now I have missed a good pun on swords and technique."

Kai almost laughed. "It's true," Ienobu added. "My father has practiced shudo well past an acceptable age. My great-grandfather made such light of him that my father eventually strangled his first partner in a bath. That very day he forced himself on ten virgins. One conceived, he took her to concubine, and I was born. My mother is now exiled to a shrine in Hokkaido. I do hope to go visit her one day."

"I doubt he's known a woman since. Masamori is the new apple of the Shogun's eye," Tadanaga added using the general's personal name. Kai was shocked at the familiar tone Tadanago used, and clearly, he was not hiding it well. Usage of a man's personal name was almost always kept to private meetings between close associates, and Kai was surprised to see Tadanaga use Hotta's so openly. It was one thing to refer to someone by his personal name in one's head, but completely different to bandy it about in conversation. Tadanaga and Ienobu laughed. Kai felt almost as if he had entered a dream world.

Importantly, though, he had found a ready source of information in the two. He ventured a second question unintroduced.

"Lord, if what you say is true, how then does the Shogun's wife become pregnant? Just a few years ago, word came all the way to us Suwo that there had been a miscarriage. We were forced to observe three days of mourning," he asked. Almost immediately, Tadanaga's look soured. His hands gripped his reins tightly, and he bit back a curse.

Ienobu answered, "My father's wife was originally promised to my uncle. They are occasionally allowed to see each other, and the child was conceived in one of those visits. My father allowed the pregnancy to progress to preserve the illusion of a happy and healthy marriage between him and his wife, but when the child was born a boy, he had it killed."

Kai could not manage to do anything for several moments other than stare at the plank floor of the cart. How much of a monster was Iemitsu? More so than Kai had known even after the events at the waterfall shrine. Neither Tadanaga nor Ienobu spoke again for several minutes.

A soldier rode from up the column leading a second horse for Kai. Kai could not help but notice that the grey horse was rather shabby and fairly old. No doubt whoever was in charge of the stables on the journey saw Kai as a piece of baggage, so he provided a pack animal for riding. The soldier handed the reins over, gave a rather disgusted look, and rode back up to his position. Kai had only ever ridden a horse once before, and that was many years ago. Perhaps it was a good thing that his mount did not appear to be capable of bolting into a gallop or bolting at all.

"Left foot in the stirrup, then a quick bounce up to an extended leg," Tadanaga offered. Kai nodded and managed to find his way into the saddle, more or less, in the first try. "Good," Tadanaga commented, but it was far from the booming optimism of his exclamation earlier.

Ienobu held out his reins as a lesson, "Pull gently in the direction you want to turn. Pull back on both to slow. Pull back more to stop." Kai smiled in an attempt to break the tension, but also to mask his own uncertainty. He felt very out of place on the horse. He preferred to keep his feet on the ground; fewer surprises that way.

Despite his initial fears, riding turned out to be just one more skill to master. It was almost like a duel in some ways. He had to anticipate the beast's desires while attempting to maneuver it into a position to benefit his own good. After a few miles, Kai found that as long as the path was straight, he did not even have to devote much thought to riding.

"You are a quick study," Ienobu stated. Kai allowed himself half a smile. He was still not certain what the end game was for these two men, but he sincerely hoped they were honest. They seemed to be, but many things seem to be and turn out otherwise.

The mood was still dour, and Kai almost regretted asking about the child in the first place. Yet, it was good to understand the depths to which one's opponent was willing to sink. It appeared that Iemitsu's limit was almost bottomless.

"Uncle, I have just come up with a joke, and I require you to judge it," Ienobu said suddenly. Tadanaga cocked an eyebrow at the youth and waved his hand for Ienobu to proceed. "My father has taken innumerable things from the people of Nihon and made them sad. But what is the one thing he could take to make all of them happy?"

Tadanaga pondered for a moment. "I do not know. What is it?" he asked.

"His own life," Ienobu said with a smirk. Kai went wide-eyed in shock. Tadanaga chuckled once, then again, then burst into such a fit of laughter that Kai feared the man would fall off his horse. He laughed so hard that he began to hold his sides, and the laughter did not subside until it broke into a fit of coughing and his face began to turn blood red. Soldiers up the processional started to turn to see what the disturbance was. One even rode back to check on Tadanaga's health. He was waved away with assurances between coughs and even more laughter.

Finally, after many minutes, Tadanaga regained his composure and his breath. "Nephew," he said with a grin, "that might be the funniest joke I have heard in my life." Ienobu beamed, and the tension of the discussion prior was completely alleviated.

They rode for several more miles, joking and exchanging stories. Kai mostly kept quiet, learning more about the two men than he offered about himself. He felt confident that they understood what he was doing, but neither the Prince nor his uncle seemed to mind. He did come up with one pressing question that he directed at

Tadanaga.

"Lord Tadanaga, what did the Shogun have Hotta tell you that convinced you to duel me?" he asked.

"My brother threatened to send me to a monastery and forbid me from entering the company of a woman!" Tadanaga exclaimed with a look of mock-terror on his face. Ienobu laughed, and Kai allowed himself a genuine smile.

That night, Kai found the limits of the trust that Iemitsu was willing to extend. He, Ienobu, and Tadanaga were sitting around a fire exchanging stories when Hotta came stomping up.

"Back into the cage with you," he demanded glaring at Kai.

"Surely, that is not necessary," Tadanaga put in. Hotta puffed up his chest and grabbed Kai by the kimono.

"By orders of the Shogun," Hotta added with a grunt. Kai allowed himself to be loaded back into the cage. Hotta seemed to take extra relish in slamming the bars and locking the chain in place. "You are not a free man," he growled at Kai. "You had best remember that you live only at the mercy of the Shogun."

As Hotta made his way off, Kai saw Ienobu watching from the shadow of a tent. The young man made his way over to Kai. "You wish to avenge your family by harming my father," Ienobu stated. It was not a question. Kai checked his initial urge to blurt out an answer. There was something about Ienobu that put his mind at ease. Kai looked at him again, or maybe for the first real time. There was an air of nobility about the youth; a potential greatness that Kai knew would be worthy of the loyalty of men. Perhaps even Kai's loyalty…

It was a gamble, but Kai answered honestly, "I do wish it, though my father, in almost his last breath, forbade me from acting rashly and getting myself killed in the process."

"Teach me well, and I will protect you for as long as I live. I will be shogun one day," Ienobu spoke with surprising earnestness. Kai did not notice that Ienobu had left the side of the cart until he was only a shrinking spot of blue in the darkness across the camp. Though he found that he could get comfortable enough to sleep, none would come to him. Too many unanswered questions challenged him. His internal arguments kept circling back to exactly how Ienobu had managed to affect him so quickly. Kai was walking down a dangerous path, but he somehow no longer felt alone.

Chapter 4

"All of man's work is a bloody business." — Yamamoto Tsunetomo

The group traveled at a leisurely pace for several more weeks. Several lengthy stopovers broke up the monotony of the road. Iemitsu was clearly conducting a personal inspection of all of the Tozama nobles. Some joined the procession on their way to Edo for the sankin-kotai. Others joined the caravan for a few days only to break away to attend business elsewhere. All the time, Iemitsu projected lordliness. If a subject had been loyal, the Shogun beamed approval and acceptance. If one had disobeyed, the Shogun's temper was quick and final. More than one of the Tozama lords lost their lives along the road to Edo. Kai was even permitted the use of his katana several times, but only to serve again and again as kaishakunin to those who had displeased Iemitsu. Each time Kai dispatched another of Iemitsu's foes, the Shogun went out of his way to praise the skill of his new servant to the Fudai lords in the processional. Kai had never in his life felt more empty. Only the admonishment of his father and the assurances of Tadanaga and Ienobu kept him going.

When he was not tasked with beheading people for the Shogun's amusement, Kai was permitted a modicum of freedom within the camp. In an effort to win over as many of the guards as possible, Kai readopted the demeanor of a household servant. He took on cleaning, cooking, and maintenance chores which, over time, began to engender good nature. The fact that Tadanaga spoke well on his behalf had seemed to make many of the soldiers' attitudes change almost overnight.

As a self-imposed rule, Kai never went within twenty paces of the Shogun or any of the wakadoshiyori, though several times he longed to rush into the fray and bring as many of the men as possible with him into death. He voluntarily allowed Tadanaga to keep his katana when he was not training Ienobu. Kai felt that the sight of himself openly carrying the blade would work against him. He saw the guard Masutomo regularly and assumed that someone had specifically tasked the guard to follow him. Kai always made a note to greet the guard, and he made it clear when he moved about the camp that he was doing so slowly enough as to not give even the slightest hint of escape or malice. The malice, Kai kept simmering deep inside himself. His father had taught him that Bushido did not allow for rashness, but revenge was clearly defined and, in fact, expected in many situations. The Shogun's time would come if only Kai had the patience to plan and wait.

As a pupil, Ienobu proved mostly competent. The boy was, as Kai had predicted, not very strong, and that hampered him with some of the motions. Eventually, Kai suggested that Ienobu use a wakizashi in practice, as the shorter blade more closely matched the boy's smaller stature. Ienobu refused and redoubled his effort to bring his katana under control. The gesture impressed Kai who, despite himself, found that he began to genuinely enjoy his time with Tadanaga and Ienobu without the nagging feeling that it was all some sort of trap. The two clearly did not share much more than a name with the Shogun, and Kai allowed himself to truly relax only in their company.

Kai's guess about the route the group would take was accurate. They had only stayed in Hiroshima for a night. Kai had only ever been to one other city in his life, Hagi on the western shore of Honshu. Hiroshima was much of the same, not much more than a castle surrounded by a fishing village. There were several such locations newly founded upon the ascension of the Tokugawa Clan. Iemitsu had chosen to visit a cousin at Fukuyama Castle, but upon seeing the state of the area declared it too dirty and moved on.

Osaka, on the other hand, was much different. People by the thousands flocked out to the road to watch the Shogun pass. There were no plans to stop in the city or even to enter it properly. Instead, the party kept to a more northerly road and passed over the Yodo River by a wide bridge clearly used to move carts into and out of the city. Even without passing through the gate, Kai felt himself becoming overwhelmed. Even the out-villages of Osaka were larger than Hagi, and the sheer number of people made him feel uneasy. Such a noise!

Vendors along the roadside shoved food and trinkets of every kind in Kai's face claiming that it was the best whatever-it-was in all of Nihon. Tadanaga and Ienobu seemed completely unimpressed with the racket and carried on as if nothing had changed from the quiet mountain roads. Kai found himself more than once having to quickly catch his breath as if he was afraid that there would not be enough air to go around.

But Kai did not truly feel the weight of civilization until they arrived at Edo. For three hours, Kai rode his horse through a clot of humanity more dense than Kai ever believed possible. Spring was full on by then, and the warmth only seemed to stir up a distinctly musty odor from too many bodies pressed too close together. What must have been tens of thousands of people met the processional outside of the city, hedging the roadside for miles upon miles. Multi-tiered pagodas marked shrines outside the city. Some were larger than the Kikkawa home in which he grew up. The shops along the road sold items that Kai had never heard of before. When the group passed the Kan'ei-ji Shrine, Kai checked his horse and simply gawked. There were more buildings in the complex than in the entire village just down the mountain from his home.

The wealth of these people was almost unimaginable. Kai saw men and women walking down the muddy sidewalks dirtying clothes that would cost more than Hidoyoshi had made in a month. Yet, there was poverty as well. Beggars stuck out bowls or cups from mats in alleyways or street corners. Many had been shooed away when the Shogun passed but had crept back out of their holes in an attempt to beg a coin from a soldier or bureaucrat.

A line of walls stood out in the distance, and for almost a mile, Kai wondered what they might be. Passing through the city had taken its toll on him, and when the walls began to creep closer, he almost started to feel light-headed. Edo Castle was the most impressive structure he had ever seen. Its walls were made of great grey cut stones and stood dozens of feet high. By the time Kai was able to make it into the broad dirt yard in front of the walls, they were all he could see if he looked left or right. Indeed, they enclosed a huge plot of land in a loop almost ten miles in circumference and contained seven different wards with distinct designs and purposes. There was a moat of indeterminate depth that separated the walls from the outer yard, and multiple bridges spanned the moats leading into several gates which sporadically broke the grey façade of the walls.

Soldiers escorted the sankin-kotai lords off to the left, across a bridge, and into one ward of the castle where several complete palaces were waiting for them. The Shogun and his personal party took another bridge and gate.

"You should do your best to memorize the route from the gate to the Honmaru," Ienobu said appearing out of nowhere and breaking Kai's awestruck gaze. "The inside of the castle is meant to confuse invaders. There are multiple sets of walls and moats, and they do not all align to make right corners. The Honmaru is where we live, and it is a fortress to itself," he added. Kai nodded, still spellbound by the size and scope of the complex's layout. As he moved through the gate and into the compound, Ienobu's words were proven more than true.

There was not one pathway or even one main pathway. Instead, paths met and diverged at seeming random intervals. Kai noticed that the ones chosen for him to follow typically graded upwards. Before long, they had gained enough elevation to see out over the rest of the castle. Kai shifted his view to the west to find that the walls enclosed enough trees to make a small forest. Off farther to the north grew an entire garden of flowers and tended shrubs. Buildings of various sizes were everywhere, but the donjon tower was clearly meant to dwarf them all. The multi-story keep stood nearly two hundred feet tall and stood as a final, and hopefully impenetrable, place of retreat in case of an enemy invasion. If Kai did not fully understand the power of the Tokugawa Clan before seeing it, he certainly did from then on.

Another moat separated the Honmaru compound from the rest of Edo Castle, and the procession passed over another bridge and through an incredibly elaborate gate. He was told to dismount his horse and continue on foot. When he lost the extra altitude, everything looked different. Despite his best efforts, Kai had lost his bearings. He could still tell the directions, but he doubted if he could recall all the individual turns he would need to make if he wanted to escape. He looked to Ienobu who had gone over to enter the residence with his father. Tadanaga was nowhere to be seen, and suddenly Kai felt very much exposed.

The feeling did not last long. Jubei came out of the retinue and gave Kai a hard shove in the back. "Come with me," he grunted. As he passed the rest of the guards, he had two fall in behind Kai with weapons at the ready. Jubei led Kai around several passages to a small courtyard in a corner of one of the main walls of the Honmaru. It was closed on a third side by a row of three small apartments. Kai guessed they were for personal courtiers for the Shogun or something of the sort. Close enough to come at a call, but far enough away that they were out of sight. Jubei opened one of the screen doors and gestured Kai inside.

The room was very sparsely furnished. A bowl for water sat on a mat just to the left of the door. Another mat against the back wall had a block of wood wrapped in fabric, which only barely classified as a pillow. The rest of the floor was dirt, and there was no window to let in any light. Without asking any questions, since Jubei's sneer did not seem very welcome, Kai stepped inside. Jubei closed the screen and ordered the guards to stand watch. Kai noticed that Jubei gave a bit too much savor in the order to kill Kai if he tried to escape. It was clear that the Shogun did not yet fully trust him.

Over the next few days, Kai fell into something of a rhythm. He taught all of Ienobu's lessons in the courtyard outside his room and saw little else. He was not permitted to wander at his leisure which kept him from being able to mentally map where he was in relation to the Shogun, or even where he was in relation to the gate. He tried to glean as much information as he could from the guards outside his room and only had minor success. Some of the guards, like Masutomo, had been on the road with him, so they had witnessed Kai's willingness to humble himself to even the lowest soldier in the Shogun's army. The others that had only met him once he arrived in Edo were much less willing to talk. It was the latter group that ignored his given name and began to refer to him as the Kaishakunin. Soon, it was all of them, though Kai held on to hope that at least a few of them did so out of something other than spite.

***

A knock at the door shook Kai from his meditation. Before he was able to move to answer, Tadanaga stepped inside. The guard followed him into Kai's room. Tadanaga laughed, "Hiroichi if this man wanted to kill me, neither you nor I, nor we together would be able to stop him." The guard nodded but did not exit the room. Tadanaga chuckled again, "Orders are orders after all."

Kai stood up and bowed to Tadanaga who returned the bow with one of his own, a very formal and absolutely perfect motion. "The day has come, then?" Kai asked.

"Indeed, it has," Tadanaga replied. Iemitsu had given his brother two months after returning to put his affairs in order in the capital before he was to be sent into the far northern reaches of Honshu under the auspices of being a loyal bastion of strength amongst the Tozama. In reality, Iemitsu hated Tadanaga and was jealous of his natural charisma. People feared Iemitsu, and his orders were followed to the letter, but the men loved Tadanaga. They would follow his slightest suggestion, even if it be to jump into a volcano. Many believed that Iemitsu secretly feared a coup by Tadanaga. Kai had heard as much from Tadanaga himself.

"It has been an honor to know you sir, and I will forever be in your debt. Were I able, I would accompany you to the North," Kai said with absolute honesty. Tadanaga just smiled. He pulled a katana out of his waist sash. It was only then that Kai realized Tadanaga had three swords at his hip.

"This is yours. My brother has expressed great concern at allowing you to wear it in the castle. I don't know if I could properly explain how much he fears you. I also don't think I can properly explain how much of a legend you have become in the city. My brother turns away challengers on a daily basis. Men have traveled from three provinces away to duel with you. You are something of a celebrity, which makes him even more uncomfortable about having you armed. Remember what I said about children with toys," Tadanaga reminded. Kai was shocked.

"The Shogun has nothing to fear from me," Kai said, trying his best to be convincing. Tadanaga looked at him for a moment with a wry lop-sided grin.

"Of course he doesn't. Why would he?" he said. Before Kai could rejoin, Tadanaga held out Kai's katana to the guard. "I did manage to convince my brother to allow me to leave your blade with your attendant. I won't be around to hold on to it, and Ienobu is not ready. I trust that you will be attending the celebration tonight?" Tadanaga asked.

"I was not aware that one was being held," Kai answered.

"Oh, indeed. A grand send-off for the loyal brother to the Shogun who is being sent to live among the traitors and heathens," Tadanaga replied in a mocking voice. "I will send for you. Ienobu will be there as well, and I have a mind to have him duel some of the guards, with bokuto of course. He will need your instruction, as I plan on being so drunk that the two women I am courting will look like four."

With no further discussion, Tadanaga left the room. The guard exited with him, and Kai moved to the door after it had been closed. Tadanaga frequently spoke to the men briefly before leaving, and Kai wanted to hear what was said.

"Hiroichi, have you considered my offer?" Kai heard Tadanaga say.

"Yes, my lord. But I would have to betray my oaths to your brother."

"Nonsense. How is it a betrayal when the lord is not loyal to his own oaths? You simply must come with me when I leave. The women there will be so tired of me after a few years, and they will need someone to console them! Besides, many of the other palace guards have agreed to come as well so you will not be alone. Did you not swear your oath to the Clan? Have you also forgotten that I am a Tokugawa?"

"No, my lord. You make an honest case. If you desire, I will accompany you into the North."

"Good!"

The conversation continued for another few moments, but Kai was lost in his own thoughts. He would undoubtedly be in the presence of the Shogun that night, and he wondered if any chance would arrive. He had agreed to train Ienobu and even found some fulfillment in doing so, but his desire for revenge still smoldered within his core. Every day he was alive was another chance to strike back, yet he knew he had only one chance. Whatever the outcome, he would not live to try again. Any plan had to be airtight, and being confined as he was, he had only slowly been able to gain much-needed information.

He sat back down to meditate on all that he had learned. Even the smallest scrap of data may be a vital cog in his machine of vengeance. He was surprised by another knock on his door. Only when he opened his eyes did he realize how long he had been lost in his thoughts. Full night had already fallen, and the guard at the door was there to escort him to the party. It was not Hiroichi, who must have rotated off duty. Instead, it was Masutomo, an incredible turn of luck for Kai's plot. He said nothing, only stood up and followed Masutomo out the door. He did not even ask to take his sword. It was not the right time for it yet.

Masutomo led Kai down several hallways and through various courtyards that the prisoner had never seen before. If the palace were truly this vast, his job would be ever the more difficult. He needed to reckon a way to get himself closer to the Shogun, and he feared that job would prove an insurmountable challenge. The first step would be accomplished that very night. Kai had pondered long and hard about how best to win the Shogun's trust and had worked out a plan just before Masutomo had disturbed him He practiced his exact words in his head, how he would say them, and with what expression on his face. He found it difficult to do so with the gnawing pit that had opened in his stomach.

When Kai arrived at the party, Tadanaga was already well on his way towards being drunk. Iemitsu sat on an elevated dais in the rear of the room and looked only slightly interested in the goings-on. Ienobu was seated just to his uncle's right speaking with an elegantly dressed woman. Her bright yellow robe stood out shockingly from the rest of the attendees who, other than Tadanaga, were dressed in more somber garb. Kai had never seen her before, but from her appearance, Kai guessed that she was Tokugawa. She was younger than Iemitsu but not by much.

Before anyone spotted Kai, he spoke softly to Masutomo, "I need to speak with the lord Hotta Masamori. It is of absolutely dire importance," Kai said. Masutomo was one of the few guards with whom Kai had managed any headway. The guard looked somewhat puzzled at the strange request.

"Can you not tell me? I will pass along the message," Masutomo said. Kai put on an urgent, pained look, but he did not respond. After a moment, the guard sighed. "Stay right here. Do not move. Do not speak to anyone else." Kai nodded.

He watched as Masutomo moved through the crowd to the back of the room. Each second brought only more nausea. He suddenly hoped that Hotta would not take the bait. Then, at least, Kai would be released from his own plot through no fault of his own. Hotta was standing, as always, behind Iemitsu. When Masutomo began speaking, the wakadoshiyori captain made a show of being perturbed. He gesticulated wildly in what Kai assumed was a stern dressing-down of Masutomo. Yet, after another brief exchange of words, Hotta stormed off the dais and through the crowd towards Kai. Kai steeled himself, there was no turning back now. Hotta began shouting when he came within earshot.

"By all that is holy, I vow to you that this will be your death if every word is not true to cause!" Hotta yelled. Kai bowed, deeply and plaintively, and began to speak. "Stand up! I cannot hear a word you are saying over this din of drunkenness!"

"My lord," Kai said, "I believe the life of the Shogun and his son are in danger. I have heard first-hand his brother gaining the allegiance of many of the palace guard. He plans to take them to the North when he goes, and I believe them to be the core of what he hopes will be an army to challenge the Lord Shogun. He has already approached me to aid him and train the other Tozama lords of the North, but I refused. He tempted me with adoption and even left my sword with the guard outside my door as further incentive. It was to be mine as soon as I agreed to aid him. I have also heard first-hand his plans to have some of these guards duel with Prince Ienobu this very night, and I believe this to be used as a cover to eliminate the heir to the throne. If both the Lord Shogun and his son were killed..." Kai allowed his voice to trail off.

"Then Tadanaga would reign," Hotta followed right on cue.

"I submit my life as payment if I am wrong. And even though I do not presume to suggest that I am capable of reasoning better than the Lord Shogun, I would have you relay to him this information. He will be able to discern the plot himself with three simple questions." Kai followed. Hotta heard the three questions, pondered for only a brief moment, and stormed back towards the dais.

Upon arriving, he reported all of what had been discussed to Iemitsu who grew visibly angrier the longer Hotta spoke. When Hotta finished, a fire burned in the Shogun's eyes. Kai recognized the body language of the Shogun immediately. He had seen it on the road to Edo when servants were disloyal and were moments from death. Iemitsu stood and shouted loudly over the party. The revelers soon recognized who was yelling and quieted down.

"Where is my brother!?" Iemitsu shouted. Tadanaga stood, though he swayed under the influence of the amount of sake he had consumed.

"Here I am, dear brother," Tadanaga answered.

"I charge you to answer me, and I will have your life if you hesitate even one second in answering!" the Shogun bellowed. The crowd seemed to understand that the tone of the party had shifted dramatically at that moment, and they parted so that the two brothers had a clear lane between themselves.

"Are you going to ask me a riddle?" Tadanaga laughed, not grasping the fury in his brother's tone.

"Have you convinced the guards of the palace to lay their loyalty with you?" asked Iemitsu.

"Only a few, not more than three quarters," Tadanaga joked.

"Are these men planning on leaving my service and going with you to the North?"

"Absolutely! Who is going to bring me my sake?" he answered. To punctuate the response, he took another long draught out of the jug on his table.

"And do you plan on having some of those very guards duel my son tonight?"

"I'm sure he'll make it out alive," Tadanaga said, choosing his words poorly. Kai looked to the Shogun, who by that point was as red as a beet.

"Seize him!" Hotta yelled to the wakadoshiyori around the dais. Tadanaga was utterly confused. He made an attempt to draw his sword to defend himself, but he was so drunk that he could not get the blade out of the scabbard. The men dragged Tadanaga up to the dais where his brother waited. They dumped him in a heap. Ienobu moved up to the dais as well, but the Tokugawa woman grabbed him by the arm and jerked him off to the side, under an awning, and into the shadows.

"What is the meaning of this?" Tadanaga questioned. He tried to stand, but the guards pushed him down again. "Keep your hands off me!" he said.

"Your plot has been revealed, brother," Iemitsu spat out the last word with contempt. "You are not going to survive the night."

"Father, what has he done wrong?" the prince shouted from the side, breaking free from the woman's grip, and bounding up to the middle of the dais.

"Quiet!" roared the Shogun, "I am not in the mood for your childish inquiry." Ienobu stood shocked and allowed the woman to draw him back off to the side. Kai could tell that she was trying to convince him to leave, pulling him towards a door. Ienobu, however, refused to leave his uncle's side.

"A plot? What plot?" Tadanaga asked.

"The Kaishakunin told Masamori the whole thing already! How you plan on taking my elite to the North to be your generals! How you wanted him to train the other Tozama to fight against me! How you planned on having my own son killed tonight! You have always plotted against me! Always courting favor with honeyed words! I have had enough, and you will die here and now!" the Shogun ranted.

"Kai said this? It is a lie! All nonsense! Kai is my friend!" Tadanaga protested.

"Is this true!?" Hotta yelled. Kai was startled, and it took him a moment to recognize that the captain was addressing him. "Did you agree to be a part of the scheme only to turn craven at the last minute?"

"No my lord. I have come to see the truth in the Lord Shogun's words to me. He has been nothing but honorable, and I have come to love him for his grace and virtue. Were it of any value, I would swear my fealty to him," Kai responded.

"Prove your words true!" Iemitsu yelled. "Take his sword and kill him where he sits condemned by his own words!"

"NO!" yelled Ienobu, and the boy tried to move to his uncle's side. The woman had placed herself bodily in Ienobu's path and simply wrapped him in a firm embrace. Kai moved through the crowd deliberately.

"If this is truly the will of the Shogun, I will gladly submit to it," Kai said to Hotta.

"Kai, why have you done this?" Tadanaga asked sincerely. Kai did not answer and did not meet Tadanaga's gaze.

"Do it!" Iemitsu commanded. Hotta grabbed Tadanaga's sword and pulled it out of its scabbard. He offered it handle first to Kai, who took the katana confidently.

"With this deed, I swear loyalty to the Lord Shogun Tokugawa Iemitsu, may his eyes look upon me with only approval from this day forward," Kai said. It only took one quick swing.

Chapter 5

"If you keep your sword drawn and wield it about then no one will dare approach you and you will have no allies." — Yamamoto Tsunetomo

Ienobu did not come to his lesson the next day. Nor did he come the subsequent day. After a week of absence, Kai wondered if he would ever see the young man again. Kai found it hard to gain information from the guards outside his door. Many of the men who had begun to show a glimmer of kindness to him reverted to the incommunicative skeptical jailors Kai had known from the mule cart on the way to Edo. Even Masutomo, whom Kai had almost thought of as a friend, refused to so much as look at Kai. Soon, Kai noticed that Masutomo was not even being stationed outside of his door anymore. Kai wondered if he had asked for reassignment.

He had expected that his condition would change if he succeeded, but he had thought that he would be allowed more freedom of movement and a higher level of trust. Instead, he was more and more cut off from the few people that he knew within the castle. The loyalty that the guards showed to Tadanaga must have been much greater than Kai anticipated. Had he managed to alienate himself from everyone?

With nothing but time to think, Kai tried to understand exactly what had gone so wrong. Ienobu, he expected to react negatively. The boy was so much more close to his uncle than his father. Kai had mentally prepared himself to lose significant standing with the prince. The handful of guards that had planned to move with Tadanaga to the north was likewise likely to hold significant grudges. But Kai had counted only a few that he knew for certain. The majority of the men stationed within the castle, he had firmly placed as supporters of Iemitsu. It was Iemitsu that Kai had clearly misjudged. Kai had felt that by ridding the Shogun of his most open, or most perceived, threat that he would be seen as a loyal servant willing to put even his own life at risk to save the legitimate head of government. He had not believed that Iemitsu would shower him with gifts or adopt him into the Tokugawa Clan, but surely he would be allowed to carry his sword and be given proper quarters. Tadanaga's words about how much the Shogun feared Kai must have been true.

The broil of Kai's emotions occupied his mind ever more as the days of solitude continued. He returned again and again to the most important question: Had he dishonored his father? Deception was not unknown or unexpected within the code of Bushido. Kai had sworn to himself that the Kikkawa Clan would be avenged against the Tokugawa Clan, and it was beyond doubt that by killing Tadanaga, Kai had struck a deep blow against his enemies. Yet, Tadanaga had offered him hospitality and never once shown him disrespect. Kai had heard his father speak multiple times about how it was the duty of a samurai to act without hesitation regardless of the outcome. Was that not what he had done? Even the noblest and worthy adversary was still an adversary. Even the closest of friends was not as important as family. He must be steadfast. Any selfless act done to uphold the honor of his sworn lord could not be wrong. He tried to convince himself that he was resolved. Only two emotions were undeniable in his mind, guilt for his actions and hate for Iemitsu.

***

A week turned into two, and the time went by without any word or sign from the outside. Kai had almost forgotten what the sun looked like. Since Ienobu was not coming for lessons, he was not allowed outside. The door opened in the early morning for food and again at dusk for food and to empty his toilet bucket. When the door opened early one afternoon, the shock of light caused him to recoil. He rubbed the balls of his hands into this eyes in an attempt to remove the dancing spots, but he did not succeed.

The visitor began to speak immediately not seeming to care whether or not Kai could even tell who it was. "I am not over fond of coming to this part of the castle, and my brother is not overly fond of you having unsanctioned visitors, so this meeting will be quick and to the point," a woman's voice said flatly. It was the kind of voice that did not offer any room for argument.

"Who are you?" Kai asked. His eyes made out the outline of a woman in a fine kimono. Her hair was done up in the same style as all of the rich women Kai had seen entering Edo.

"I am Tokugawa Masako, Iemitsu's sister. I am married to the former emperor Go-Mizunoo, and my child Meisho currently sits on the Chrysanthemum Throne as Empress of all Nihon," the woman spoke as if Kai should have already known that. Kai made to respond, but she held up her hand. "You do not need to say anything just yet. I have come to speak to you on my own behalf, and I need to be direct. I do not need your pawing affection."

Kai had not meant to imply that he was offering any affection, but pointing it out did not seem like the best course of action at that moment. He could not make out enough of her face to tell if she was glowering at him, but her tone and her body language left no room for doubt. She paused for a moment, and he felt as if she was working herself for something. When she finally launched into it, Kai could only hold on for the ride.

"You orchestrated the death of my brother, Tadanaga, and for that, I am honestly sad and rather perturbed. I had such high hopes for him. If you had not meddled in the plans of your betters, I might already have Iemitsu's head on a spear adorning the walls of Honmaru. Yet you show up here with the pomp of a celebrity when you are nothing more than a bumpkin from the hill country and throw chaos to the wind in some sort of ill-planned revenge scheme. Honestly, I am surprised you are still alive. Do you not understand that Iemitsu suspects you even more now? No, do not answer yet, I am not finished," she barked. She took a breath, then another. Then she began again with even more anger than Kai believed possible.

"You have ruined so much. I am now forced almost back to the very foundations of planning, and you do not understand anything. If only Bushido allowed for more common sense, you men would not constantly get in the way of better judgement and sound thinking. Instead, you just wave around your katana. I have but two questions now, and I expect that you will answer them directly and pertly," Masako said, fuming. Kai had made out her appearance somewhere in the diatribe and found that she was the woman at the party that tried to constrain Ienobu. He nodded to her to continue, as it was the only thing he thought profitable at the moment.

"Does your plan of vengeance include spending Ienobu's life the same way you did Tadanaga's?" Masako spat.

"No," Kai said before he could even register. His heart had supplied the word without his mind giving thought, but Kai found the answer to be true nonetheless. Even though he had not seen Ienobu in weeks, he still felt a strong connection with the young man.

"Is there anything that I can say or do to put you off your quest to punish my brother?" came the second question.

"No," Kai said again. This time both his heart and his mind spoke in unison.

Masako stared at him for several moments. "Well, at least you understand pertness. I will not have you killed, and even though I speak freely to you, you should not count me as an ally. My only concern is the life of my daughter, and Iemitsu stands as the biggest obstacle to her living to old age. If I deem it necessary to speak with you again, I will make it happen. Otherwise, do not try to contact me via any means. You are not part of my plan, but you may yet be enough of a distraction for mine to work.

"And just in case you feel the need to tattle on me like you did Tadanaga, I offer you this: You will never hate Iemitsu more than I do. You did not grow up with him. You were not brutalized by him. And you will never know the lengths that I will go preserve my family. Iemitsu knows that I am coming after him, and all it would do was prove to him that you are not trustworthy," Masako said. She nodded at one of the guards, and the door slid shut again.

Kai was completely befuddled. How many webs of intrigue ran through the palace? Was anyone truly loyal to anyone else? Kai had never been around many women in his life that were his superiors since Hidoyoshi's wife had died before he was born, but none of the women of rank he knew spoke with such a force of will. He was both impressed and not sure how he needed to respond to the knowledge that Masako shared.

***

Several days more went by, and Kai was no closer to understanding the strange interaction. If anything, Masako stating that she would not have him killed had made him feel even less secure than before. The ramifications of the statement were almost impossible to fully work through. All he had been able to determine for certain was that no one, save perhaps Ienobu, could be trusted. It was all too much to track.

Kai was once again deep in thought when a knock at his door startled him into awareness. The door opened, and a man entered. He was dressed in simple clothing, but Kai immediately understood that this man was important. Kai decided that he would not move from his seated position and he would not be the first to speak. He had to be so much more careful now that he doubted his own ability to plan. A single stray word could be the end of him. He must not forget that he was a prisoner, and again, there was no way to determine on which side this man pledged his loyalty.

A guard came in and placed a mat on the floor of the cell and a cushion on top of that. The guard left without saying a word or even looking at Kai. The man sat down on the cushion and began to look Kai over. The man was middle-aged, perhaps 50. Though his face was creased with many lines, between his unkempt brows, on his forehead, and at the corners of his lips, the man radiated a vibrancy that was undeniable. He wore simple, nondescript clothing of charcoal grey with no device or mon. His eyes were such a dark shade of brown that they appeared almost black, and when Kai met the man's gaze, he saw the wisdom of many more than fifty years within them.

They sat for many moments in silence, neither showing the willingness to break eye contact. Kai felt like a pupil being silently scolded by his master for shoddy work or poor behavior. He began to wonder exactly who this man was, why he had come to Kai's cell. His mind raced through option after option, but none seemed to fit. Had Masako changed her mind? Or was this Iemitsu's bidding?

The seconds dragged by, but the man sat perfectly still and stared. He appeared unarmed, but Kai wondered if that were true. Was the man here to put an end to the unwelcome houseguest? Upon that thought, Kai immediately began to size up his possible opponent. He felt confident that he would be able to overpower him. Kai tensed but immediately tried to hide it. The man simply stared on.

It took Kai some time to realize what was actually happening. This was a duel. It would not be fought with swords, but with words. Once he understood, he also knew that he had already lost. That was the lesson. It was time to admit his defeat if for no other reason than to act subservient. He still knew neither this man's purpose for visiting nor with whom his allegiance lay.

Kai moved into a kneeling position. The rustle of his clothing broke what had been absolute silence, shocking Kai at how loud it was. "You have beaten me, my lord," Kai said.

"What was the lesson?" the older man said with so little inflection he betrayed not even the slightest emotion or intent.

"Not every battle is fought with a weapon. There are those which are fought with the mind." Kai replied. This was a lesson that he had learned in the past, but he had evidently forgotten it. He understood much then. His time in the dark had dulled him. His anger had made him ignorant. He needed to be more careful lest he betrays something he could not explain.

"You show promise, but you have much to learn," the man said. "Ienobu will return to his lessons tomorrow. You will teach him the way of the blade to the best of your ability. If you truly wish to have your revenge, I caution you against rash action. The Shogun is quick to anger but slow to trust. You will never come close to him by ridding him of enemies. He sees everyone, great or small, as an enemy. You would have to kill the world, and by doing so, you would expose yourself."

Kai found no words to respond. This man, whoever he was, had deconstructed Kai in a matter of moments. Kai's entire mind was an open book, and this frightened him. "Am I so transparent?" Kai asked plaintively.

"You claim to be a servant, but you still do not bow," the man said. And with those words, he stood up and moved towards the door. Kai sensed an opening. He fought with himself for a moment, worried about giving away too much to an unknown entity, but the man was only one step from the door. He had to try something. He decided that it was best to move in on a tangent to try to hold as much back as possible.

"Did Masako send you?" Kai asked, hoping for any additional pieces of information.

"No, and you should not speak her name. She is not on anyone's side but her own, and she is both predictable and unpredictable because of that. Many in the court are sympathetic to her cause, and there are many who spit at her passing. You will not get to the Shogun through her, but your attempt to keep me talking succeeded.

I will answer only one more question before I leave. And once I leave, I will have to decide whether or not I trust you enough to speak with you again. So you had better make it a good question," the man responded earnestly.

Could this man read minds? Either he could, or Kai's assessment of his own intellect was woefully inadequate. As soon as the thought crossed his mind, he remembered how badly his last plan had gone and confirmed to himself that his opponent's wit outmatched his own in this discussion. If he was to understand who this man was, he might as well start at the beginning.

"Will you not give me your name, Lord?" Kai asked. It was a simple question, but honest.

The man stopped, took a moment to contemplate the question, and then stooped over. Using his finger, he wrote several kanji on the dirt floor of Kai's cell. "This is my name," he said. Kai locked down a flush of embarrassment before he once again gave himself away. Yet, even the slightest of actions seemed to be as clear as an unclouded sky to the other man. "I think I will see you again. After Ienobu leaves tomorrow, I will visit. In time, I will teach you to read what I have written. Your skills with the blade are evident, and you understand that you are still lacking. There is no true learning without arms and no true arms without learning."

With that, the man knocked on the door. The guard opened it from the outside, and the man left. Kai felt in his gut that he needed this man's help. Kai felt a sort of kinship with him. If he was not an open enemy of Iemitsu, he must at least be an ally of Ienobu. Was that not close enough? The guard must have come in to remove the mat and cushion as well, but it was many hours before Kai recognized that they were gone.

***

When Ienobu arrived the next day, Kai prepared himself for what would likely be a very uncomfortable lesson. Kai had not slept at all. The words and lessons of the man refused to allow him to sleep. Yet somehow, his mind felt sharper than it had in many days. Kai walked out of his room, retrieved his sword from the guard but then thought better of it and handed it back over.

Ienobu was already standing in the courtyard, waiting for his erstwhile teacher. Kai knew what lesson he needed to teach today. He approached the boy but stopped with some distance left between them. Appraising his student's countenance, it was clear that he was distraught. He seemed caught between wanting to run away and cry and wanting to rush Kai with his blade drawn in an attempt to gain retribution. "If you must try to kill me, do it now," Kai said.

Ienobu flinched, and his hand went to his katana hilt. He began to vocalize a noise halfway between a moan of pain and a growl of rage. "Do it!" Kai barked harshly at the boy. The younger man drew his blade with a flash and with three quick strides closed the distance between them. He slashed right to left at Kai's waist then reversed and slashed again. Kai deftly moved out of the way. Ienobu tried an upward slice, then a downward one, followed by a stab back up at Kai's face. Kai could see every attack well before it happened and did not allow the boy to strike him. The guard at Kai's door moved up to the edge of the stones that marked the border of the courtyard, but Kai held a hand up between swings to stop him. For two whole minutes, Kai allowed Ienobu to attack, and the boy's strength and endurance soon flagged.

Eventually, the boy dropped his katana and collapsed into a heap on the broad flat pavers of the courtyard. He sobbed with great heaving breaths. "Why?!" he yelled at Kai.

"You know why, and no words I say will remove what I did or the guilt that I feel from it," Kai responded.

"Do you hate my father so much that you would murder an innocent and honorable man?!" Ienobu yelled back.

Understanding that he had an audience, Kai had to play his role. "I do not hate your father. He has been nothing but honorable to both my family and myself. The fact that I am alive now is only at his grace and mercy," he said.

Ienobu looked at his teacher with abject disgust. "My father's grace and mercy be damned." He stood on shaky legs, gathered his katana, and tried as hard as he could to storm off.

Kai watched him go. He turned to go back to his room, but a voice called to him, "That went well." Kai turned to see the older man from the day before standing under one of the covered porticoes off the edge of the courtyard. He had clearly witnessed the entire scene and had kept to his word to visit Kai.

"He needed to learn, just as I did, that anger alone is impotent,

Sensei," Kai said thoughtfully. The older man nodded.

"So, you have decided to call me Sensei? Well, if I am to be your teacher, let me teach," he said as he produced a small writing table from around a corner. He walked to the center of the paving stones and put the table down. On it were several items: a brush, an inkwell, and several scrolls of paper. He sat down directly on the stones and gestured for Kai to sit across from him. Kai moved over and sat. The stones were hot, and though they were mostly worn smooth, they were hard and irregularly shaped. Kai shifted to try to find a better seat.

"You are supposed to be uncomfortable," Sensei admonished. Kai immediately stilled himself. "Good." The teacher picked up the brush, dipped it into the ink and then looked Kai in the eye. "We are going to write a poem."

Chapter 6

"Wisdom comes from paying attention to wise people."
— *Yamamoto Tsunetomo*

It took several sessions with the teacher for Kai to begin to feel even the slightest bit comfortable. Kai listened greedily and spoke like a miser, but Sensei was far too skilled in conversation to give away anything he did not want to release. Kai could sense goodness in the man, but his motives were still clouded. Ienobu spoke little to Kai and refused to answer questions. For several days, Kai understood that the prince had only come to train because Sensei made him.

Kai found that learning to read was both more and less difficult than he had believed. There were so many characters to remember, and Kai frequently mistook them when they were on their own. It was actually easier when there was a passage from which he could infer the meanings of the words he did not know from the ones he did. He made steady progress, but there was an itch at the back of his mind that never quite went away. For all he was learning, he was getting no closer to understanding Sensei or fulfilling his vow.

In what was likely the seventh or eighth visit from Sensei, Kai could no longer contain his curiosity. "Will you not tell me your name, Sensei?" he asked again.

The older man smiled. "You have shown rather remarkable restraint. I did not think that you would last the week before cracking. Congratulations on beating my estimate. I am not often wrong when I judge people," he answered. Kai bit down on an angry outburst, that immediately caused him to feel embarrassed over yet another lost point in their on-going duel, and he resorted to putting down his brush and sighing. Sensei moved the writing table out from between them and placed a hand on Kai's shoulder. "I am not your enemy," he said. Kai felt the honesty, but he no longer trusted his own ability to judge.

Sensei sat back and crossed his legs. "I see that I have once again misjudged you. I have never been trapped against my will, and I have never lived under threat of death for as long as you have. I was wrong to keep you guessing for so long, and for that, I apologize," he said.

"You were wrong, you say? Why should I trust your apology any more than a stranger's? I do not even know your name," Kai responded skeptically.

"Well, I guess it is time to answer questions then. For the record, though, I gave you my name when we first met. You just have not made an effort to ask me what the kanji read. If you were wise, you could have asked innocuously for one or two of the symbols every other lesson and over time worked out what it was. I have purposefully steered you away from those on the floor of your cell during our lessons," the man responded. Kai could not bite back the curse at that revelation. He shook his head in disbelief.

"Do not be so hard on yourself. I am on your side, and we share the same goal. Iemitsu must be stopped or contained," Sensei said. Kai immediately turned to the guard by his door who was undoubtedly close enough to hear what Sensei had said. He half expected the guard to draw his weapon and strike the older man down where he sat on the pavers. "He is one of Masako's men. Do not worry about speaking to me in front of him," Sensei explained with a shallow laugh.

Kai thought better of trying to deny he felt the way he did about Iemitsu. Instead, he pressed for a further explanation. "Why do you feel that way?" he asked.

"I follow the teachings of Confucius, and paramount among those teachings is the belief that Heaven has given each of us a role to play. Some are called to follow, and some are called to lead, but each must work to do so as well as possible. Only then will the will of Heaven be made true on earth. Iemitsu knows this or claims to, yet he does not live accordingly. He is brash and pompous. He acts impetuously for no other reason than his own amusement. He has forgotten why his grandfather fought to unify Nihon.

"Ieyasu was not perfect, but in his heart, he knew the suffering of the people, and he knew that peace was the only way to alleviate it. Hidetada was at least intelligent enough to listen to his father after Ieyasu retired, but as soon as Ieyasu died, he developed too many fool-hearted desires. Iemitsu was flawed from the beginning, and he is pushing Nihon back into the same state of fear his grandfather tried to eliminate. Peace is only peace if it is not enforced by fear. Would you agree?" the man asked. Kai could not produce an answer. He felt like it would take him days to digest what Sensei meant.

"It is difficult to understand. Allow me to simplify it. I serve the will of Heaven, and Iemitsu acts against everything that I believe. His son, on the other hand, possesses the qualities that I believe a good leader should. If you do not trust anything else that I say, trust this: Ienobu should rule and Iemitsu should resign as his father and grandfather did when their times were right," Sensei explained.

"I agree," Kai added. It was a dangerous admission, but he felt like he was safe in making it. Such was the conviction in Sensei's speech that it set Kai at ease, finally.

"I think that is enough for today. I will see you again tomorrow after Ienobu's lesson. Teach him well, and do not doubt that you can play an important role in the future of our world. Revenge against Iemitsu can be obtained by more ways than the katana," Sensei added.

***

The next two months passed like a blur for Kai. The subsequent lessons with Ienobu had been less emotional and more productive, but Kai felt that the prince would never fully forgive or trust him again. It surprised Kai that the loss of Ienobu's friendship stung him as badly as it did. Yet he had been brought to Edo as an instructor, not as a friend. Twice, Hotta had personally sat in on the lessons. He had said nothing, and Kai was sure that he was there under implicit orders to observe and report everything directly back to Iemitsu. Kai suspected that his speech to Ienobu had made its way through the guard to the Shogun, as his meals had grown in portion and variety and he was allowed proper bedding.

Sensei came every day as well and sometimes visited in both the morning and in the afternoon. It had taken Kai two more weeks before he was able to read the kanji the old man had written on the floor of his room. He asked each day for one kanji in the name, but Sensei did not give up the information all at once. Kai learned to be content with asking without knowing. Until he managed to collect

59

each symbol, he had carefully avoided that corner and made certain that nothing disturbed the characters almost as if he were tending a shrine. When Kai finally read the name Hayashi Razan, he almost could not believe it. His Sensei was the private tutor and advisor to the Tokugawa shoguns and had been appointed by Ieyasu himself. No wonder Sensei had been able to bring Ienobu back into lessons with Kai. He was Ienobu's sensei as well. When Kai had pressed Razan on why someone so important would spend so much time with someone so unimportant, Razan had simply replied, "I do not know why you continue spending time with me. Should I go?"

Once Kai had wrestled with that lesson and understood its meaning, he had refused to call Razan anything other than Sensei. He had already proved his wisdom many times over. As Kai's trust in Razan grew, Kai began to speak more about his past and the mistakes that he had made along the way. Razan listened intently and offered many good words of advice. "By being ashamed of your mistakes, you make them crimes," was a frequent refrain. They were the words of Confucius, and Kai found some solace in them. His Sensei knew many such sayings but was not always willing to speak them. At times silence was the best teacher, letting Kai work out the problems in his own head. Razan always seemed to know which way was best.

Before Kai reckoned the time that had passed, it was time for the noble lords who had served their four months of the sankin-kotai to return to their homes. Summer had arrived, full and hot. It would be miserable traveling in the humidity, and Kai did not doubt that Iemitsu had planned it that way. Razan and his teenaged son Hayashi Harukatsu were to travel with the lords, and Kai was surprised when his Sensei suggested that both Kai and Ienobu accompany the party. Kai doubted seriously that the Shogun would even consider that a realistic option. When Hotta arrived at his door to take him to the throne room, Kai suspected only the worst.

There were three sections to the main palace in the Honmaru. The outermost court was for the Shogun to meet with what he believed to be the general riff-raff. Courtesans, ambassadors, and such. The next was for ranking lords and where the daimyo and Shogun conducted most of the important business of the realm. The innermost chambers were for the Shogun and only his closest advisors. This was where he planned, or plotted, and thought. This was the beast's den. And that was where Hotta directed Kai.

When he entered, Iemitsu was kneeling at a low table looking over a map. On it were lines demarking the provincial boundaries of the islands of Nihon. Across from Iemitsu, Razan spoke in quiet tones pointing to several different locations as if describing a travelling plan. The teacher came to the end of a sentence and gestured toward Kai and Hotta. Iemitsu stood and walked towards them. Hotta dropped to kneel, and a stir went through the entire room as Kai did the same. A look of utter bemusement crossed Iemitsu's face. He looked back to Razan as if to see if the old man had planned this as some sort of practical joke, but Razan looked just as shocked as everyone else. Though the guards at the door were too well trained to gawk or break their stillness, their eyes, however, were wide in amazement.

"And what do we have here?" Iemitsu asked between sincere chuckles. Hotta swatted Kai in the side, and when Kai looked to the captain, the other man gestured with his chin towards Iemitsu. When Kai did not immediately interpret the motion, Hotta mouthed 'Answer him.'

"My lord, you have a humble servant, that is all," Kai answered plainly. This brought another round of chuckles from Iemitsu. Kai wished for nothing more than to burst forward, disarm Iemitsu, and then use the Shogun's own blade to relieve his body of his swollen and rotten head. There would be no way Kai could survive. Hidoyoshi's words rang in his head, and Razan had shown him a new way. Patience and supplication were rewarded more than obstinacy by those who thought too highly of themselves. Iemitsu likely believed that everyone should kneel simply out of awe of his person, much less out of the honor of his station.

"Well this is quite the turn of fortune, is it not? I had heard rumors that you managed to get over the loss of your family. I do appreciate all of the work you have done with Ienobu, and I have not forgotten who exposed the plot of my brother. Still, though, a shogun must be cautious when wielding the weapons at his disposal lest he cut himself on his own blade. Don't you agree?" The final question was loaded with so much false sweetness that Kai could only nod from the floor. Had he spoken, his voice would have no doubt given him away.

The Shogun looked to Hotta, who seethed at any positive remark directed towards the Kaishakunin. "Did I not say that he would come around sooner or later, Masamori?" he asked. Hotta did not answer, and Iemitsu just chuckled a bit. "Get up off of the floor, the both of you," Iemitsu said. Kai and Hotta rose, and Iemitsu went back to sit at the table with the map. "I am told that you have been meeting with Hayashi Razan and that he has even succeeded in teaching you how to read. Is this true?"

Kai composed himself. His life, and more importantly his revenge, depended on an increasingly difficult string of longshot chances. He did not have the luxury of even one mistake. "Yes, lord. He has taught me many things. To read was important, but more importantly, he helped me understand my role. If I am to be of any service to Heaven, I must play my role to the best of my ability while on earth," he replied trying his best to sound penitent. Iemitsu looked to Razan and then back to Kai.

"My teacher is indeed wise, and it appears to me now that he may even be able to work miracles. But, that is yet to be seen. He will be escorting several of the lords back to their homes, and he has asked for my son to accompany him. I had already decided to do so. There is wisdom in allowing my son to act in my stead, as the lords will one day bend the knee to him. Hotta will act as my military representative on this trip and with him will be one hundred of my personal bodyguards. Another two hundred men at arms will travel in order to dissuade any brigands and ensure the safety of the party. I wonder if you should be allowed to go with them..." Iemitsu pondered.

Kai did not rise to the bait. He understood that any eagerness would betray his plans, and he also knew that he was not actually supposed to answer. He stood still and quiet. A dozen heartbeats passed. Iemitsu put his hand to his chin in a clear attempt to look lost in thought. The Shogun eyed Razan, who did not give any committal response. He looked to Hotta, who seemed close to boiling. Then he looked directly at Kai. "I think that we might be able to work out an arrangement. I would hate for my son to be without his famous instructor for two whole months," he said almost as an afterthought.

"My lord..." Hotta began. Iemitsu simply held up a hand to quell the protest.

"The Kaishakunin will be remanded into Masamori's personal care. My general will be in sole, personal, control for the duration of the trip. Not even my son shall overrule him in any matter dealing with this one. All have heard, and all will obey. That is, they will obey if they are truly my servants," and with that, the Shogun waived a hand for Hotta and Kai to leave. The two men began to exit, but Iemitsu spoke up again, "Oh, and Masamori, do try to bring the Kaishakunin back at least mostly alive, would you?" The general nodded grimly, and the two men exited the chamber. Kai began to make way back to his room. Before he was three steps out of the door, Hotta grabbed him and slung him up against the wall. He pressed his forearm into Kai's throat and leaned very close.

"I do not for one second believe your charade. I do not believe what you said about Tadanaga. And I do not believe that you earnestly bend the knee to Tokugawa. You may have fooled my lord, but I have not forgotten my vow to protect him. If you so much as breathe out of line, I will flay the skin from your bones with your own sword and leave you as sport for the birds. Test me on this, and no amount of your skill will save you," he growled through clenched teeth. Without allowing Kai a chance to respond, the general pushed him roughly down the hall. Kai only smiled.

***

The trip itself would likely encompass two months but might stretch into three. If that was the case, the weather might force the party to winter in the south. The snow had been difficult to predict in the last few years. Spending months in the south was not ideal for Tokugawa supporters. Many of their most outspoken critics, especially the Mori, held sway in the southern provinces. The plans were to accommodate the Fudai lords before the Tozama, as only seemed right. Hotta relegated Kai to walking, as Hotta had noted that he was no samurai deserving of a horse. Kai was not bothered with walking, but he did miss the opportunity to ride again. He was also next to last in line and prohibited from wearing his sword. An armed guard walked behind him at all times. As a gesture of kindness, or so Hotta had said, Kai, carried a bokuto for defense. Kai felt comfortable of his own ability; at least while he was awake. And there was the bonus that Hotta was not be forcing him to sleep in a cage the whole trip.

Date Masamune was first to be escorted home. The Tokugawa had greatly expanded his domain which was just over a week's journey from Edo. His castle Kanran Tei looked out over the water at Matsushima. The man was easily in his middle sixties, but he still rode straight and strong. If legends lived and walked among men, Masamune was one. At camp one evening, Razan had told Ienobu, Kai, and a growing group of others stories about the past glories of the loyalty and bravery of the old man.

"I have heard men say that he lost his eye in a duel with an oni," Ienobu said with a laugh.

"He suffered a sickness when he was young that robbed him of most of the sight in the eye. When his teacher remarked that it would always remain a hindrance to him in battle, Lord Date Masamune plucked the eye out with his own hand," Razan said. "That is how he gained the nickname Dokuganryu."

Ienobu laughed, but then suddenly quieted. "My uncle would have made much sport over the nickname One-Eyed Dragon." He stood up and walked quietly to his tent. Kai made to follow him, but Razan motioned for Kai to stop.

"Let the boy work out his feelings alone. You would do nothing but make it worse," the Sensei stated matter-of-factly. Kai sat back down.

In an attempt to change the subject, Razan's son, Harukatsu interjected, "I cannot wait to see the pine-covered islands at Matsushima. I hear that they are quite impressive."

"I have seen them once before, and they are indeed spectacular. We will see many things on this journey that are beautiful, but we must also be mindful of how we can learn from them. From the islands at Matsushima, we can learn that even the most ambitious feat of determination still has very real limitations that it cannot overcome despite all effort. The pines thrive on the islands despite the rock and scarcity of soil. They grow tall, and some grow horizontal out from the very walls, but they are confined by the water. Think on that tonight," Razan said looking directly at Kai.

The next few days passed in quiet contemplation. Ienobu did not come to the fires and took his meals alone in his tent. He also did not take his lessons when the company stopped at midday. There was much time to think. Kai understood what Razan had meant, though he did not want to admit it. The Sensei would likely not approve of Kai's whole plan. Kai was not sure that he had the skill, or the heart for that matter, to accomplish his goals, but the fire burning in his belly refused to allow Iemitsu to go unpunished. One thing had finally been made clear in Kai's mind; Iemitsu's death alone was not enough to balance the scales.

Upon receiving Lord Date back to the castle, the people had thrown a great feast. The old lord gave a booming speech with a voice that defied his age. Kai was not allowed to participate in the castle and planned on spending the next two days enjoying the scenery from the beach. The ocean water was already too cool to swim in, but Kai found that he enjoyed conducting drills while calf-deep in the waves. The motion of the water threatened to pull or push him off balance, which forced Kai to focus on his center of gravity and his feet placement.

He also hoped that Ienobu would see him in the water and be drawn down to the shore for a lesson. The second afternoon, Kai walked down a narrow dirt path that led out towards the water. The castle was situated on a slightly elevated peninsula overlooking a wide bay. The path cut down through a small bluff to a narrow beach on the south side of the bay. Boats, mostly smaller fishing vessels, made their ways out to the deeper water in high hopes. Scattered throughout the bay were dozens of islands, some large enough for buildings, some so small that only two or three trees were able to find purchase.

Kai took off his sandals and unwrapped his feet. This place was truly beautiful. The pine-covered islands dotted the bay at irregular intervals. His Sensei was right, there were lessons to be learned. Kai wondered how long Razan had known that Kai felt like a pine tree trapped on a small island.

He had been staring for an indeterminable amount of time when a voice disturbed him. "Well worth the trip into enemy territory," the man said. Kai turned to see him standing up on the bluff beside the path, not five feet from where Kai sat on the beach. Had Kai been so lost in contemplation that he did not hear his approach? Or was this man simply a ghost? The man was in his late forties. He had long scruffy sideburns and a thin mustache. His hair was unkempt, and his clothes were rumpled and travel-stained. The jacket was natively brown, but his kimono might have only appeared that way from the dirt. At his side, he wore two swords. His wore no family mon, and Kai could not find any trinket or symbol to give away the man's origins. He could have been from anywhere. Or more accurately, it may be that he was from nowhere.

"You are not a friend of the local clans?" Kai ventured. The man snorted a laugh.

"I am not a friend of the Tokugawa. They refused my service years ago. I am on my way as far south as I can make it. I travel to Kyushu, but I wished to speak with Hayashi Razan one last time. He is a good friend, and one worth making a trip so far north to see. I doubt I will ever come this far again. I hope to spend my remaining years in quiet contemplation. And as it seems that I have disturbed yours, I do humbly apologize," the man said. He bowed deeply and began to walk away.

Seizing an opportunity, Kai made a quick decision. "My lord," Kai said, standing to move back up the bluff to meet him. The man paused and turned.

"I am no lord, and I no longer have a lord," he said. Kai accepted the correction in stride.

"We are traveling southward ourselves, and though my party is full of Tokugawa supporters, I am not one of them. I am only in their service, but I am sure I could arrange for you to join us," Kai said. He was not sure if it was a valid claim, but he had made it anyway. What luck to find another friend of Razan in such an unlikely place? Any enemy of his enemy, regardless of how shabby he seemed, was not an asset to discard out of hand. Something about this man, though, made Kai believe that he was more than he appeared.

"My friend, I would only bring more trouble than you desired. Once I was made known to be traveling with you, there would be an endless line of challengers slowing you down," the man said. "It is best for me to be alone, though I am truly honored by your invitation."

"I understand the weight of skill. My father, Kikkawa Hidoyoshi, and my brothers were never able to remove the burden. In the end, the skill of my father as a teacher was what brought him to his end," Kai said quietly. Upon hearing the name of Kikkawa, the man straightened.

"You say that Kikkawa Hidoyoshi was your father, but he and his sons are all dead. I have heard tales from the Suwo Province of their seppuku in submission to the Tokugawa," he said.

"It was their only honorable option, and what you have heard is true. I am not the son of Hidoyoshi by blood, but I sat at his table and called him father," Kai responded.

"You are the Kaishakunin," the man said flatly. Kai nodded a single time. "Then you should come with me, friend. Back to the south. Away from the Tokugawa. There is a place where you can escape your adversaries and find peace, but it is far from here."

"I cannot leave until my vengeance has been made full. I believe that you will understand that," Kai said. The man put a knowing hand on Kai's shoulder, nodded firmly, and then turned away.

"If you ever change your mind, you come and find me. I believe we have more in common than you truly understand," he said as he was walking away.

"Sir, how would I find you? For what name should I ask?" Kai asked skeptically.

"I am called Miyamoto Musashi," he said over his shoulder. "I will not be hard to find."

Chapter 7

"If one you thought was your friend keeps his distance from you during trying times then he should be considered a coward." — Yamamoto Tsunetomo

The first challenger appeared just after the party had passed into the Asada Domain on the southward leg of their trip. Kai had expected that he would continue to be sequestered from outside contact as had been established over and again by Iemitsu. Hotta had different plans. He had Kai dragged up to the front of the line and presented him to two men. One man was close to Kai's age and was presented as Aoki Shigekani. Aoki spoke for the other man who was introduced only as the court sword master.

"If you want your man to duel the Kaishakunin, you must agree to several terms," Hotta said. "As the Kaishakunin claims to be the best swordsman alive, he will fight with his bokuto regardless of what weapon his opponent chooses." This was patently false, but Kai knew better than to correct Hotta in front of another noble.

"The duel will also result in death. Either the Kaishakunin will die, or he will act as his namesake requires at the seppuku of his opponent," Hotta added smugly. Kai flinched at the thought. He had experienced enough at the deaths of his brothers and father. The other nobles he had to second were easier emotionally, but his mind had revolted at the idea of being a toy for Iemitsu. Tadanaga had also fallen to Kai's blade or more accurately, he thought, to his deceit. Kai was growing tired of death and had no desire to duel. His studies with Razan had even begun to make him question the role of violence in his plans for vengeance, but his family honor demanded retribution. It might be that more deaths would be needed for him to be whole, but this man was not one of them. Kai wondered if Hotta understood much of his mood. If so, the general was doubly evil.

"Lastly, if your champion loses the duel, you will pay a fee of one thousand koku of rice in next year's taxes as a penitent gesture to delaying our journey needlessly," Hotta finished. He crossed his arms over his chest and thrust his chin out at the younger lord. Kai had reached the point of absolute disgust. This was clearly extortion, and such a large amount could feed one thousand people for an entire year. The Aoki Clan was not particularly rich, though they were very noble, and so much in recompense would surely make the lives of their people harder. But they were Tozama, and Hotta seemed to relish the possibility of punishing the outsiders.

To make matters worse, by making such a spectacle of the Aoki Clan's challenge, Aoki was almost certain to accept or lose face in front of the other southern Tozama lords in the retinue. The other daimyo had moved up to the front of the column to watch. Ienobu and Razan stood just behind Kai, but he could not tell if they would back him if he tried to refuse. If he turned to catch their gaze, Hotta would likely become more suspect of Kai's relationship with his sensei. Aoki looked resigned, but he nodded his assent to the deal. Hotta chuckled deeply. He gestured for Kai to come forward and spoke with a quiet but menacing tone.

"If you are truly loyal to the Tokugawa Clan, this man is your enemy. His family fought against your lord, and he believes that the glory of his clan is greater than that of yours. I cannot kill you directly, but rest assured if you do not fight, if you choose some path of noble sacrifice, that man there will cut you down without mercy. And what service is a dead kaishakunin to his lord?" Hotta spoke as if he were explaining a lesson to a child.

Kai boiled on the inside. He doubted greatly that the man would pose much of a threat. He was armed with a long-bladed odachi, a blade more suited to horseback combat than dueling. There was little chance that this would end in anything other than seppuku, and Kai would be denied the honor of a victory in the duel by the immediate shade of beheading his enemy. Kai refused to give up his life with his vengeance unfulfilled and for the glory of no one but Hotta, and that meant the Aoki swordmaster must die. In his mind, Kai stumbled upon another option. If he were able to offer his opponent a death in battle instead of seppuku, all parties might retain their honor. And so, Kai decided, against his own will, what he would do.

The man drew his odachi from his back and lifted the blade directly out to point at Kai's face. He gave a small smirk of confidence. Kai pulled his bokuto out and held his arm out to his side, parallel to the ground. "Begin!" Hotta yelled.

Kai took a breath to still his mind. Gazing into his opponent's eyes, he knew immediately that he had won. He took a step forward to put himself within striking range. The swordmaster gave no ground and pushed his blade out further, hoping that the distance granted him by the length of the odachi would keep Kai from being able to attack. Kai swung his bokuto quickly across, knocking the long blade out to the side. Then, in the same motion, he pushed inside his opponent's guard and drove the butt end of his bokuto into the man's throat with a sickening crunch.

The man dropped his odachi and began to scratch at his throat. His face turned a sickening shade of reddish purple. He tried to gasp for breath, but he was unable to manage. Within a moment he had fallen to his knees, wet gurgling noises coming from his mouth. Kai returned his bokuto to his waist sash and bowed to his opponent. Hotta erupted.

The general lashed out with a gauntleted fist and struck Kai directly in the temple. Kai neither expected the blow or saw it coming, and it landed with full effect. There was a brief moment of free fall, and then Kai was on the ground. Before he blacked out, Kai heard a cry of surprise from Ienobu.

***

Kai was lying on his back. The surface on which he was lying bounced irregularly. He felt almost like he had detached from his body. Then the noise began. First, a thin whistle in his ears that sounded like it was a mile away. Then it grew louder, almost to the point of becoming unbearable. He tried to lift his hands up to cover his ears, but he could not move. After several agonizing moments, the whistling died away, and the noise of the processional replaced it. He heard the crunching of gravel under booted feet, men talking to each other, and the creaking of wooden wheels.

He opened his eyes, slowly because the light was so bright. His left eye opened most of the way, but his right refused to budge more than a sliver. Above him, he saw the branches of pine trees. The dark green fronds stretched from the right and left to form a tunnel of sorts. He tried to speak, but all he managed was a ragged and guttural moan. "I think he is waking up," he heard someone say. He turned his gaze up just enough to see Ienobu, who was riding on the rail of the cart. Kai felt a dip in the bed, and a thump as another person boarded. The figure of Razan appeared on the rail beside Ienobu.

"You should not move, and you should not try to talk," the sensei told Kai. "You are in very bad shape, and I believe you lucky to be alive." Razan looked off to one of the men in the processional and shouted for water to be brought to the cart. After receiving the container, Razan dipped in a small bamboo tube. He slowly offered the mouthful of water to Kai who was unable to move up much and had to sip slowly through swollen lips.

"Masamori struck you many times before I had to remind him that my father wanted you alive. He was angrier than I had ever seen him be. He has not stopped his grousing about how you dishonored him, and even now I suspect he plots against your life," Ienobu stated.

Kai was not surprised. He had known that it was a risk to dispatch the man in the duel. That was not what Hotta wanted, and he knew that Hotta would likely react petulantly. Kai had never suspected an outright beating. He had guessed wrong again.

"Where?" he managed to rasp out.

"You have been unconscious for three days. We are now traveling in the Tango Province to return Lord Kyogoku Takahiro to his castle on the other side of the Amanohashidate land bridge," Razan answered. "You need to rest. Do not try to move. We have bundled you up to keep you steady while on the road."

Kai did not have the strength to argue. He slipped back into sleep.

***

The next week was a fog spent wavering along the border between painful consciousness and restless unconsciousness. It had taken another two days before Kai even felt strong enough to move from his back up to a sitting position in the cart for a few minutes. The rush of lightheadedness that met him once he managed to get upright another day after that caused him to pass out. Had Razan not been there to catch him, Kai would have fallen flat on his face. Kai had never hurt so much in his life, but he refused to show it. Hotta would be punished both for the beating and the constant threats from before. Kai's father had once told his pupils that threatening an opponent was akin to drawing a katana without the will to strike. A true samurai kept his tongue sheathed allowed his actions to speak on his behalf. Hotta's lack of decorum was a shame on his own house and the Tokugawa.

Razan noted the way that Kai glared at Hotta and admonished him quietly, "Timing and rhythm, Kai." Kai understood the lesson, but it burned him inside. By the time that the processional reached the edge of the Choshu Domain, Kai had taken to spending the majority of his waking time feigning sleep in the back of the cart. With his eyes closed and his body still, he allowed his mind freedom from distraction. In his meditation, he came up with iteration after iteration, imagining every scenario into the seventh and eighth order of repercussion. He folded plot into scheme all the while forcing his mind to calm. His revenge was nothing but a protracted duel. Once he allowed his mind to clear, the strikes and parries of his attack came into focus. One thing became apparent: Hotta needed to be removed.

Feeling refreshed, and somewhat recovered from his beating, Kai was able to walk on his own through the gates of Hagi. Kai remembered two things most clearly about the city. First, he remembered his initial trip to the city with his father and brothers. He had only been nine or ten, and the size of the city had impressed him. Now that he had been through cities that actually qualified as large, he recognized Hagi for what it was; not much more than a glorified fishing village. That brought him to the second thing he remembered, the smell of fish. The whole city smelled of it, mostly because you could not escape the water anywhere you went. The city hugged the shore of a bay and spread itself out in a crescent shape around it. If Kai's nose had not been so swollen, he had no doubt the smell would be there.

This leg of the trip was somewhat unexpected, as no Mori lord was in the party. Ienobu had warmed back up to Kai after the duel, and Kai spoke to the young prince who rode his horse at the rear of the processional to be near his instructor. "What business have we in Hagi?" Kai wondered out loud.

"My cousin, Mori Hidenari rules here. The old lord, Mori Terumoto married my father's sister. This was not the aunt that you have met but another one. My father did not publicize this stop. I believe Masamori is here in an official capacity to gauge the level of discontent amongst the Mori. I have heard my father's side of the story, but I have grown to understand that he sees the truth through his own filter. Will you tell me why the Mori hate the Tokugawa? Didn't you grow up here?" Ienobu asked.

"My father was of the Kikkawa Clan who are sworn hatamoto of the Mori. Before the Battle at Sekigahara, the Mori sent my father's cousin Kikkawa Hiroie to your great-grandfather to communicate their willingness to sit out the battle. A bargain was struck and promises made, but the terms were not met afterward. Tokugawa Ieyasu claimed that it was a warrior's duty to fight, and he punished the Mori Clan for its apparent cowardice. They were pushed out of Hiroshima and Aki to Hagi. And though they were still punished with the loss of land, your great-grandfather, Gongen-sama, seemed to treat the head of the Kikkawa Clan with less anger and held nothing against the lesser nobles of the house including my father. This only served to further humiliate and infuriate the Mori, and they did everything they could to bring Kikkawa low. My father only survived on his earnings as a swordmaster. The Mori have not forgotten, and I have heard that every year they meet to determine if the time is right to overthrow the Tokugawa," Kai spoke lowly.

"They would not stand a chance," Ienobu said, almost regretfully. Kai had seen the armies of the Tokugawa, and he unfortunately agreed. The clash would bring destruction upon both Clans, but the Tokugawa would not be utterly destroyed. Kai sensed an opening and decided to change the topic.

"You mentioned your aunt, Masako," he said, leaving the ending open for Ienobu to speak as he desired.

"Are you asking me if you can trust her or if I understand her?" Ienobu answered deftly. He looked at Kai and smiled knowingly. "The answer is no for both questions. Make no mistake, she is more of a family member than my father is, and I love her as much as someone can. But she has always aspired for more. When she married the emperor, there was great fanfare. My father did not care for someone other than himself holding the attention of the people, and her sharing our family name only made it worse. He all but forced her and Mizunoo off the throne. My cousin, who is only a child, is empress, but she is not safe. When my father wants imperial approval for actions, he has taken to blackmailing my aunt. She would prefer that I rule, but I wonder how much of her desire is based around what is best for her and not what is best for me."

The two spoke no further as they moved through the bustling business district of the city. Hagi was a port on the western shore of Honshu and made most of its wealth through fishing, though the Tokugawa had encouraged trade to grow as well.

Boats from foreign countries brought in exotic goods, and Hagi was one of only a few locations where the Shogun allowed such a practice to exist. Iemitsu was wary of the Chinese and even more wary of the Europeans. The Portuguese had brought firearms which the Tokugawa had used to devastating effect, but they had also brought their faith. The Europeans were initially successful in converting natives to their strange religion, but this soon drew the ire of the government. The Tokugawa developed a special dislike for the Kirishitan and their single god. Iemitsu's father had almost succeeded in rooting the religion out completely. The Dutch were mostly harmless, but they were also not nearly as useful as the Portuguese. Kai knew all of these things from gossip around his village, but he had never seen a European. He honestly did not desire to. He had heard that they all had hooves for feet, but he doubted that was anything more than port gossip.

There were also boats leaving Hagi, bringing rice and other essentials to the island of Kyushu to the south. The Mori Clan had grown the city, even though profiting from trade was not viewed with as much honor as more traditional means like farming. No doubt this was a constant stinging reminder of the Tokugawa betrayal. Kai had never understood allowing an openly antagonistic clan like the Mori to oversee trade with outside groups that you also did not trust. Having some interaction with Iemitsu made the reasoning a bit clearer. At least all of his enemies were in one place.

Kai had been here several times before as a boy, and overall he could not see much change. He did manage to catch a whiff of fish, and judging from the look on Ienobu's face, he was experiencing it full on. Merchants called out their wares to attract customers, and everything was covered in a light patina of grime. Kai felt more at home than he had in a long while. The cleanliness of the palace at Edo was almost unbearable. Even his cell, or apartment as he had grown to call it, with its dirt floor was still kept meticulously clean.

Just before the gates to the Mori palace, the retinue passed a small road running down a hill to the edge of the water. At the end, there was a strange building. It was built directly on top of a pier making it rather narrow, but fairly long. Kai wondered if it was a temple, but as he gained a better perspective, he understood the purpose of the structure. A large wooden cross adorned the façade, and men and women of various ages were moving into the front door of the building. It was a Kirishitan church. Kai noticed that Ienobu had checked his horse down to a stand-still. The young man stared intently at the church, and Kai recalled his pupil's interest in religious shrines.

A very beautiful teenage girl helped an elderly man pass the party on the road. She bowed to Ienobu as they passed and greeted the young lord. Ienobu, stirred from his intense examination of the Church almost fell out of his saddle when his eyes met the young lady's. Kai saw an unexpected opening.

He spent a moment lost in the deepest of thought. Somewhere along the road to Hagi, Kai had finally worked out his plans for revenge, and there was a chance here for gains to be made. Iemitsu must be made to suffer, and then, when death would be a welcomed relief, it must be denied. To accomplish that goal, Kai had accepted several difficult realities. But could these Kirishitan offer him ironic salvation from himself? It was worth the risk to find out.

"Would you like to go inside?" Kai asked Ienobu. The young man was off his horse and into the mouth of the path before Kai was able to register. He lashed the reins of the prince's horse to the gate of the path and began to move as quickly as he could to follow. His right side had been pummeled, likely by Hotta's booted feet, much worse than his left, and his limbs were still very sore.

As Kai was catching up to Ienobu, he saw the boy initiate conversation with the two who had passed in before them. "I am Takayoshi Akemi, and this is my grandfather, Takayoshi Michio," the girl said, "he is the priest of our congregation. We are going to mass."

"What is mass?" Ienobu asked sincerely. Kai found it amusing that his pupil had been so startled at the sight of the Akemi but had forgotten the girl's beauty as soon as she began to speak about her religion.

"It is one of the most holy sacraments of our Church. It is a communion with our Lord, Jesus." Michio answered warmly. Ienobu seemed to be enthralled, a sponge waiting patiently to absorb any and all facts willingly shared.

76

"But, my grandfather, Hidetada, outlawed your faith. How do you still practice so openly?" Ienobu asked. At the mention of Hidetada, Michio visibly recoiled in both fear and recognition.

The old man said as he fell to his knees. "My lord, please, if you have come to finish the job started by your grandfather, I beg that you take me alone. The congregation is small and were I not here to lead it, I doubt it would survive. If blood must be spilled to prove penitence, please allow me to offer mine," he begged.

Ienobu was so shocked at Michio that he just gawped about without finding words. He finally looked to Kai, almost begging for an interpretation. "He believes you are here in an official capacity to complete your grandfather's work. The Tokugawa Clan spent many years hunting and exterminating Kirishitan," Kai offered.

Ienobu reached down and pulled Michio off the ground. "I am not my father, nor am I, my grandfather. I came here out of genuine interest, and I mean you no harm. I have searched out sacred sites all over Nihon, and I have met with holy men of many faiths, but I am ignorant of yours. I simply sought knowledge," he spoke evenly. At that moment, Kai saw in his student much of what makes men follow their lords.

Before the conversation was able to continue, a booming voice cut through the air, "What are you doing!?" Kai recognized Hotta's growl without even turning to view him. The general was stomping down the path, his hand straying to the hilt of his katana.

With an edge that Kai had never heard before, Ienobu shot back, "I am having a conversation with these two, and you are interrupting as usual!" Kai could tell that Hotta was just as taken aback by the prince as he was. The blustering general stopped his half-assault, and his sword hand fell back to his side.

Hotta replied with an acidic edge that verged on insubordination. "My lord, these Kirishitan are not a wholesome lot. Some say that they are cannibals and purveyors of blood magic. Your family did great service to Nihon in an attempt to rid our shores of their kind. I must insist that you continue on into the palace. Your cousin has set a feast in your honor, and it would shame him if you arrive late."

Ienobu looked to Akemi and Michio. He spoke quietly enough that Hotta was unable to hear him, "I will send my teacher, Hayashi Razan, to the gate of the palace tonight after the first watch. If you meet him there, he will escort you to me. I apologize for the lack of decorum, and I hope that the general has not desecrated your sacred space." Akemi nodded. For a moment, her eyes met Ienobu's again, and Kai could recognize in Ienobu an interest in more than just the faith of the Kirishitan.

Ienobu turned and began to walk back towards the palace, "Come Masamori, let us meet my cousin," he commanded. Something in the prince had changed through this encounter. Kai felt pride in his pupil, but more importantly, Kai was relieved. The prince had discovered some new fortitude. He had proved himself to be more independent than Kai had believed possible. If Kai were able to ride the momentum of this change, he would be able to avoid the most sickening part of his plot for revenge. It was the part that went against his word to Masako and his own personal will. Honestly, the interaction with Hotta had offered Kai more relief than the days of convalescence in the back of the cart. If Ienobu could be convinced to seize the throne and rule, Kai would not have to kill him.

Chapter 8

"A warrior should be careful in all things and should dislike to be the least bit worsted."— *Yamamoto Tsunetomo*

Kai was escorted, under arms, to a small hut that was not much more than a storage room for gardening implements and tools. There was a bedroll and a bowl of cold rice on top of a barrel, and Kai took this as it came. He had grown well accustomed to the ire of Hotta, and he had long since adapted to eating little or nothing. Even when the Shogun increased his daily allotments, Kai had kept his meals small. He always held back as much as he was able just in case he was forced back onto starvation rations. Or if no food came at all. Iemitsu was fickle at best, and Kai saw it wise to prepare for whatever came.

He rolled out the bamboo mat, picked up his ration, and sat down cross-legged. As he idly picked at the rice, he tried to evaluate the extent of his recovery. The ribs along his right side had almost certainly broken under Hotta's assault. Razan had done his best to set them and wrapped a binding of linen around Kai's chest to stabilize them. Luckily, those seemed to be the only broken bones. Kai's arm and leg were both deeply bruised, and he still ached at a deliberate or quick movement. His face was a mess of bruises and swelling that had not completely gone down. But despite his physical maladies, he was strangely content. The incident at the Kirishitan temple offered so many new opportunities and removed truly distasteful ones.

A quiet knock at the sliding panel door startled him. Kai did not recall finishing his rice, though he must have at some point because nothing spilled when he dropped the bowl in surprise. The hours had once again melted away as he ran through plot after plot. He recognized briefly how much more thoughtful Razan had made him. So much less impulsive. He stood and opened the door. The hut was so small he didn't even need to take a step.

Razan and a smaller, hooded, figure greeted him. Before Kai was able to ask the meaning of the visit, he saw Ienobu move out of the garden and towards the hut. He smiled as he understood. This was to be a starlit rendezvous. "Good evening to you Kai," Ienobu said. To that point, Kai could not ever remember the prince calling him by name.

"I see we have a visitor. May I assume that this cloaked figure is Akemi-chan?" Kai asked. The young girl moved back her hood and looked at Kai with a bemused smirk.

"I was not aware, my lord, that we were such close acquaintances," she replied.

"I was not aware, my lady, that I was a lord," Kai responded. Ienobu smiled broadly when he saw the young lady. He made a motion towards the door. "I regret that my humble dwelling will not easily accommodate a party of four. Perhaps we can sit in the garden and talk," he suggested. Ienobu nodded, and the four made their way back around the hut. Perhaps ten paces away, there were two benches with a moveable lattice screen meant to block either the wind off the water in the winter or the sun in the summer. Kai moved it so that it offered the most privacy from the rest of the palace and took a seat beside Razan. He began looking back towards the wooded hill on the far side of the walled compound that housed the palace. It was a fair night, if not a bit stuffy for a city so close to the sea. There was a full moon out, and the night was fair and bright without even a hint of wind.

Ienobu immediately beset Akemi with all manner of questioning about the beliefs and practices of the Kirishitan. Razan and Kai tried their best to be silent and unobtrusive chaperones. "I believe that he might be interested in more than spirituality," Razan whispered low to Kai. Kai nodded slowly.

"I see the wisdom in this observation, Sensei," Kai added with a lopsided grin. It had been many long weeks since Kai had felt anything other than hatred. The last few days on the road had been especially painful for him, both physically and mentally, as he wrestled with his own decisions. He had come to value Ienobu, and only his rage against Iemitsu had overcome those warm feelings. He refused to allow his desire to spare Ienobu's life lead to optimism or even hope. Those ideas would only dull his resolve if worse came to worst. Still, he was encouraged that he was able to feel more than pain, more than the void left by his father and brothers.

Some time went by. Razan and Kai sat in silence, content to listen to Akemi explain her faith. Kai could not help but find some virtue in the foreign religion, much the same way he felt about Buddhism. His father had raised his family in a very traditional, city dwellers would call it rural, Shinto household. Kai was familiar with the belief as a child, but he had felt a stronger draw to it after the death of Kikkawa Hidoyoshi. Perhaps his father's spirit was watching over him.

Razan shook his elbow to get his attention. "I apologize, Sensei, I was lost in thought," he said peacefully. Upon surveying Razan, though, he sensed something wrong.

"There is no wind tonight," Razan said in full voice. He did not shout, but the words shattered the peace of the moment nonetheless. The old man pointed to the tree line behind the wall. The branches of the trees closest to the wall dipped almost imperceptibly as if some invisible force moved them.

"Shinobi," Kai understood immediately. He shot up, drawing a fiery ache down his leg, moved quickly over to Ienobu, and grabbed the prince by the upper arm. "Move!" he commanded in a voice that brokered no resistance. The prince yielded, and Akemi followed in their wake. Kai covered the distance back to the hut in just seconds. His muscles screamed at the exertion, and ultimately, the onset of a cramp saved his life. He lurched sideways as his leg refused to flex, and a black-feathered arrow lodged itself into the side of the hut where Kai would have been.

He fell to the ground, half out of instinct and half out of pain. Razan had likewise gone to the ground, pulling Ienobu and Akemi down under him. Akemi screamed when an arrow barely missed Kai's shoulder and thumped into the ground just in front of her face. Kai crawled to the door panel and threw it back. Using his body to shield the two teens, he crammed them inside. He looked to Razan, "You have to go rouse the guard." Razan, immediately understanding that Kai would not leave his two charges, ducked around the corner of the hut. Using it as cover from the tree line, he began running and yelling back towards the palace.

Kai paused just long enough to recall a mental picture of Ienobu. The boy had arrived in the garden that night without his katana. Through the door, he called to Ienobu, "Arm yourself with what you can! Tell me what you see!" Kai heard the sounds of rummaging from inside the hut.

A muffled voice returned, "There are only hori-hori and kusakichi! How are we to defend ourselves with garden tools?" It was a valid question, but a rhetorical one. Kai crawled around the edge of the hut to try to break the line of sight to the trees. One arrow grazed passed his forehead, opening a cut that began to bleed profusely. He did not give time to worry over whether or not the arrows were poisoned. He knew they likely were. He rounded the corner and took a moment to right himself. Feeling the blood already running down, Kai ripped off a piece of his kimono and wrapped it around his forehead. He knew a fight was coming, and he could not risk blood running into his eyes. A few breaths later, he peered around the corner and saw four dark shapes drop out of the trees and begin moving swiftly towards the hut. Kai knew he had only seconds before the four men were upon him, and he allowed himself only a moment to replay the scenario in his mind. The shinobi were not after Ienobu; no arrows had been directed at him. These men were after Kai.

"Do not come out of the hut regardless of what you hear. If you have anything, I can use as a weapon to spare, quickly throw it out the door!" Kai yelled into the hut. The bamboo wall was not completely solid, and Kai could see the two as dark shapes moving inside. Akemi was sobbing quietly, but to her credit, she responded quickly. The door of the hut opened bare inches, and a kusakichi dropped to the ground. The tool was not much more than a small one-handed sickle used for cutting away weeds and roots. Kai inched down and took it anyway.

Thirty yards from the hut, the shinobi split into two teams. They meant to force Kai out of cover to pick him off with their bows. Kai focused his breathing, calmed his heart-rate, and acted. The area between him and the right pair of shinobi was clear of cover. To the left, the garden offered some sanctuary. He simply hoped it offered enough. No one would be fool-hearty enough to rush the shinobi head on across an open distance when he had the hope of cover. That was exactly why Kai took off to his right with as much speed as he thought he could muster.

The pair of shinobi paused for two seconds, stunned that their quarry was so bold. They reached for their bows only managed one shot each. The first arrow shot past Kai's head, the second caught him in the upper chest, almost in his right armpit. The thick wrap of linen holding his ribs in place broke the impact just enough that the arrow did not hit bone, but the razor-sharp head cut into the already sore muscle. Kai plucked the arrow from his chest with his left hand and tapped a previously unknown reserve of strength to put on a burst of acceleration.

The shinobi pair dropped bows and began to draw swords. The one on Kai's left was quicker and managed to unsheathe his wakizashi before Kai was on him. The shinobi arced the blade towards Kai's injured side. Time dilated, and Kai saw his opening. He gave way to the blow, spinning to his left. Using the force of the spin and his momentum, Kai slammed the arrow point in his left hand into the sword-wielding shinobi's neck. In the same spin, Kai swung the kusakichi in his right arm up into the gut of the second shinobi who had just managed to extract his sword from its scabbard. It did little damage, but it bought Kai precious seconds.

The first man gurgled out a wet noise before both of his hands went up in a vain attempt to stop the flow of blood. The second staggered back put a hand to his side and readied his blade. Kai's right hand betrayed him, unable to hold on to his makeshift weapon. More arrows came whizzing past Kai. The other pair of shinobi had cleared the garden and the hut and were taking aim. He stumbled as he tried to dodge incoming fire and tried to close the distance between himself and his closest opponent. His left hand found purchase on the hilt of the fallen shinobi's wakizashi, and he opted to act defeated. He slumped to the ground face forward and feigned a swoon.

The shinobi did not offer him quarter and moved to eliminate his target. He spun his blade over for a two-handed downward stab into Kai's back. Just before the blade found purchase, Kai rolled and brought his scavenged blade up into the shinobi's chest with his left hand. The man hit the ground with a wheeze and would be dead within seconds. With both of their comrades defeated, the second pair of shinobi began to cover the distance firing arrows as fast as they were able. Kai rolled the dying man on top of him as a shield and began to search for other weapons. Arrows thudded into the shinobi's body and the ground around him. Kai had to act! The man's pack contained various thrown weapons, but Kai did not trust his accuracy throwing left-handed. His right arm was going numb, likely due to poison on the arrow tip. He did not have time to light a smoke bomb, and he doubted it would do much good anyway. Where were the guards?!

He cut his eyes up to his rapidly approaching opponents and saw Ienobu rushing the men from behind, a hori-hori in each hand. The hoes were nothing more than pointed V-shaped spades meant for turning over dirt with blades that were barely four inches long and not very sharp. Regardless, Ienobu stalked the men, quietly gaining speed. He leaped the last few feet and buried both hori-hori into the back of one of the shinobi. The man went down in a heap, stumbling into his companion and causing the man to drop his bow. Ienobu swept out the fallen man's wakizashi and squared off with the last remaining shinobi. Kai forced himself out from under his human shield and staggered towards the two. He had to get there first. He doubted that Ienobu was ready to face a fully trained swordsman.

The shinobi brought a chopping attack down on Ienobu's blade. Kai could hear the impact over the throbbing in his head. His forehead wrap had come dislodged, and blood poured down into his vision. The prince's grip on the handle was shaken by the blow, and he staggered back to regain his footing. The shinobi did not relent and came back down again with a chop. When Ienobu blocked the attack, his wakizashi clattered to the ground. Methodically, the shinobi raised his arms again, clearly meaning to disable the prince in order to finish the job with Kai. With a flash, Ienobu darted into the man's guard, and producing a third hori-hori from his waist sash, stabbed it with all of his might into the shinobi's neck. A spray of blood and a wet cough later, the shinobi fell over dead.

The first of Ienobu's victims appeared to have regained some strength and tried to raise up to crawl away. Kai arrived in time to stop him, delivering a kick to the man's face that sent him back down. Kai knelt down behind the man, pulling one of the hori-hori out of his back. He pulled the shinobi up into a sitting position and stabbed the blade into the man's kidney. The shinobi burst out in a scream, but Kai held him in place.

"You are going to die. This is in no doubt. Your wounds are fatal, but you could survive for many hours before you expire. I know two places that I could stab you with this blade to produce even more pain than you feel right now," he said. To remind the shinobi, Kai twisted the hoe so that it widened the wound. The man screamed again.

"I will end you now if you speak a name. Tell me who contacted you," Kai hissed into the shinobi's ear. True to his code, the man refused to speak. Kai extracted the second hori-hori, reached around to the front of the shinobi, and pushed the dull blade into the man's chest just under his collarbone and behind his sternum. He pulled up a bit to put tension on the nerve, and the shinobi cried out in a thin and ragged scream of pain.

"Tell me who contacted you! Was it Masako?!" Kai bellowed over the man's scream. The shinobi, bound by secrecy, was trained to endure torture. Kai knew the man would likely die before divulging any information. He heard a loud ruckus and looked up to see armed men rushing out of the palace and into the garden carrying draws weapons and torches. At their head, strode Hotta Masamori. Time was running out. If Hotta took this man, Kai would never know the truth. He twisted both blades and dragged them back and forth to cause as much pain as he could. The shinobi cried out in the most pitiable sound Kai had ever heard.

"WHO?!" Kai demanded. The shinobi, finally unwilling to endure more torture, simply pointed at the men approaching through the garden.

"The... general..." he whispered hoarsely. Kai withdrew the blade under the man's clavicle and stabbed it straight into the shinobi's heart. His foe was dead in moments. Kai slumped back, and for the first time in what seemed like hours, he looked at Ienobu. The young man had apparently closed the door of the hut and returned to Kai's side. He had witnessed Kai torturing the shinobi, and Kai could not tell if the look of disgust that Ienobu wore was for his teacher or for his opponents. He had heard the shinobi's confession. The only thing that Kai knew for certain was that he would never again think of Ienobu as a boy.

"What is the meaning of this?!" Hotta hollered as he arrived on the scene. The guards fanned out into a protective formation around the prince and Kai.

"We were attacked. These men made an attempt on my life, and Kai was the only reason that I survived," Ienobu spoke flatly before Kai had a chance to answer. It was a bold-faced lie delivered in such a way as to forestall any attempt at questioning its veracity. Hotta looked visibly shaken by this revelation.

"I see. I must make a full investigation," Hotta replied. "If the kaishakunin had anything to do with this, I will see him dead before sunrise." Ienobu moved up to the general. Though the prince was a head and a half shorter than the older man, he spoke with the authority of someone twice his size.

"Did you not hear me? I said that the only reason I am alive at this moment is the skill and bravery of that man," he said pointing at Kai. "He had nothing to do with this, and is in severe need of medical aid," At that he motioned for two soldiers who immediately went to fetch a surgeon. Hotta made to stop the men from going, but Ienobu took a step closer. He was barely a hand's breadth from the general. "You listen to me Hotta Masamori, you have far exceeded your station on this trip. The very next time I feel that you have been even the slightest bit insubordinate, I will see you dead before sunrise. Do you forget who is Tokugawa here?" Ienobu demanded.

His words seemed to hang in the air like humidity, making it difficult to breathe. The soldiers in Hotta's retinue, all sworn servants of their daimyo, seemed to experience a moment of previously elusive clarity. Above their daimyo was the Shogun. And Ienobu would one day be the Shogun. Their daimyo had gainsaid their future leader. Ienobu was right to scold a wayward servant in such a way. Kai wanted to yell that all men were fallible, even Hotta, yet he doubted his words would have the desired effect.

A soft sob came from the garden hut. Before either Kai or Ienobu could respond, a guard had thrown open the door and pulled Akemi into the light of the torches. "The Kirishitan!" Hotta exclaimed. "They must have been behind this attack!" Clearly, he knew that he had to create some fiction as a cover. He also clearly did not know that both Kai and Ienobu knew the truth. "Take her into custody!"

The soldiers moved to encircle Akemi, but Ienobu called out, "She was here with me. She has nothing to do with the attempt on my life." The men paused and looked to Hotta. He seemed frustrated that his orders were not immediately followed.

"My lord, you just met this girl earlier today. Are you certain that she played no part in this? At the very least she should be questioned, but of course, I am at your command," Hotta replied. The soldiers stood transfixed between action and inaction. Ienobu looked to Kai, who wished instantly that the prince had not done so. Kai's head was swimming, trying to keep the pieces of his plan in place, and trying to maintain consciousness. The numbness in his arm had spread through his chest and up the side of his neck.

Ienobu looked around to the soldiers who offered no aid. Kai wished he was in any shape to counsel the young man in his decision. If the fiction was to hold, Ienobu should act suspicious of everyone involved. If he refused to allow Akemi to be questioned, Hotta might suspect that the prince knew more than he was letting on.

"If she is to be questioned, my father will be the one to do it. You will not be present, and I will make all of the arrangements once we return. If Akemi will agree to these conditions, she will travel back to Edo with us unbound and free. If she does not agree, she will be treated as a noble hostage and offered every possible convenience. What say you, General?" Ienobu asked. It was a fair request, and if Hotta tried to refuse, it might be seen as casting doubt on the ability of the Shogun to judge the truth. Hotta was already shaken by the prince's newfound determination, and Kai knew Hotta was a patient enough tactician to give up ground in the short term for a long-term gain. At the moment, Hotta stood to lose not only his position but also his head.

"These terms are acceptable," he said. With the situation defused, Kai began to drift off into oblivion. Someone began to remove his kimono and the linen wrappings, but blackness closed in over his vision. His next to last thought was that he had experienced this feeling far too often of late. His last thought before unconsciousness caught him was how proud he was of Ienobu.

Chapter 9

"Above all, one should not divide one's way into two."
— *Yamamoto Tsunetomo*

Kai was in the cart again. It took far less time to recognize where he was the second time. He tested his arms and legs and was able to move all four, though his right arm tingled like it had been asleep. He slowly pushed himself up into a sitting position against the front wall of the cart. It took a moment for his eyes to adjust to the light, and when the spots finally faded, he saw Razan riding beside the cart softly chuckling.

"Perhaps you should try a bit harder to stay alive, my friend," Razan said between chuckles.

"I thought I was getting better at it," Kai replied with a smile, "I feel much better this time." He wiggled all of his toes and flexed his fingers. He did feel much better. Clearly, the rest had helped him recover from both his first and second brush with death. "What was it this time?"

"Poison of some sort," Razan replied. His voice turned unexpectedly serious, "You are very lucky to be alive. We are not certain the type, but had it been puffer fish toxin, we would not be having this conversation." Kai sobered at the thought. Poison was such a cowardly way to kill. It was devoid of honor.

"What took you so long?" Kai asked, trying to clear a foul taste from his mouth.

Razan rode a bit closer, produced a small jug of water, and offered it to Kai who gulped it down greedily. "Hotta. It seems he was already expecting some sort of fight because he was conveniently out patrolling with a full escort of soldiers. He insisted on notifying the daimyo before taking action, claiming that if he needed to take command of Mori soldiers, he must have clearance or risk insulting the local lord. It was as clear of a stall for time as I have ever seen. I

89

immediately suspected foul play, and Ienobu's report only confirmed my suspicion," the teacher explained.

"How is he? I am concerned. He killed a man for the first time and followed that by watching me interrogate the shinobi. I do not know if he was ready to experience that," Kai said. Razan nodded. He waited sometime before responding.

"Ienobu is no longer a boy and is no longer a prince-in-training. I have seen very much of Tadanaga in him in the past few days. You were asleep for five of them, by the way. He confessed to me just last night that he had been wrestling with the event in his mind. I believe that he has had the lesson of command thrust upon him in full instead of in parts. He understands death now, that is for certain," he said solemnly.

"And of me?" Kai ventured. He could not decide if he were more afraid that Ienobu would reject him as a brutal villain or embrace Kai's example and become one in his own right.

"He understands how important it was for you to have that information. He also understands that the attack was designed to eliminate you and that Hotta is now just as much of a threat to him as he is to you. I know your fears, Kai. I do not believe he will fall into his father's shadow. Ienobu is good at heart. Iemitsu was cruel from his first breath. I will warn you, though, let him broach the topic of what he saw you do on his time. Do not force him to respond until he is ready lest his fear and anger make him hasty," Razan replied.

"Where is he now?" Kai asked. He half expected to see the prince sitting on the rail of the cart like the last time.

"He rides in the procession in the position of daimyo," Razan pointed, "and beside him, Akemi." Kai looked over to see Ienobu riding, straight-backed and proud, but ever looking over to Akemi. The two were evidently in a conversation. Razan noticed Kai's reaction and provided answers before the questions arrived. "Oh, I do believe he is very much in love," the teacher said. "And I am rarely ever wrong in matters of the heart."

"Do you think it is wise to let him get involved?" Kai asked.

"I do not think that there is anything that we could do to keep him from getting involved. The connection was already there, and though there will be bitterness in the inevitable parting, I see no harm in letting Ienobu have a few weeks of happiness," Razan put in. Kai was not so sure.

"His father will never allow it," he added darkly.

"I know, but Ienobu committed himself to bring her before his father. To try to undercut him here might break his resolve. No, I think we need to allow this to play out without too much meddling from over-cautious advisors," Razan responded. It was the first time that Kai had ever called into question Razan's reasoning, and he was uncomfortable because of it. Yet, he was more unsure of what Iemitsu would do when he found his heir in love with a Kirishitan. He doubted that he would be able to shake Razan loose from his opinion, so he decided to change the subject.

"Where is Hotta?" Kai asked, searching the processional. It was much easier to do so since all of the other daimyo had been returned to their homes. Kai also noticed that some of the soldiers were missing.

Razan chuckled again. "Ienobu commanded him to wait a week before he left Hagi. I think the prince wanted to ensure Akemi a fair hearing before Iemitsu. You have taught him well," he said. It was indeed a sound tactical decision. Kai remembered his father teaching a lesson on how observing an opponent's stance in order to know if the time was right to attack. If your opponent was firmly planted, it was wise to move around to change the angle of attack.

"We will need to talk. The three of us. There are many things to plan," Kai said. Razan agreed. Things had changed, but the plan remained the same. Despite his various injuries, the threats and attempts on his life, and the constant rage that simmered just under the surface, Kai felt confident for the first time in many months.

***

The journey back to Edo was mostly uneventful. Summer was slowly slipping into Fall, and the troupe was fortunate enough that a light breeze kept the air light instead of clammy. It had reached the time of the year where afternoon rains were more common than not. The fame of the Kaishakunin was clearly spreading. Several lords brought men to challenge Kai along the way, but Ienobu allowed Kai to decide on his own whether or not to face the men. Taking a lesson from the best teacher that he knew, Kai agreed to face all of them as long as they fought with bokuto. None of them took more than two moves to defeat, and Kai left all of them with two lessons: one in swordsmanship and one in humility. The duels fascinated Ienobu. Kai would frequently have to spend an hour breaking down how he knew to make each move. It was almost the only time Ienobu spent without his attention on Akemi, who did not care for the duels at all.

There were many talks with Razan and Ienobu. Razan seemed to need the company more than he wanted to admit. His son, Harukastu, had left the company shortly after Kai had regained consciousness. The young man had fallen quite hard into wanderlust and claimed that he would not rest until he had seen the most beautiful views in all of Nihon. Akemi was present as often as not, but the men never openly plotted in her presence. Ienobu was quite taken with the young girl, and she seemed to be able to ignore her situation through a mix of bravery and trust in Ienobu's assurances of safety. Kai found her presence pleasant, but he worried that she might end up being more of a distraction than Ienobu realized. There was limited enough time to plan.

He needed to try to explain to her the gravity of the situation, so one night, after Ienobu had gone off to sleep, Kai went over to her tent. He expected to have to wake her, but he found her kneeling and praying. He waited for her to finish, not wanting to disturb her communion with her god. "Lord thank you for this opportunity. I sit in the presence of the next Shogun because of your foresight and grace. Give me the right words to say, and this land will come to know you when Ienobu takes command," she said quietly. She finished the prayer with a strange hand gesture that Kai could not interpret. When she moved to her bedroll, Kai cleared his throat quietly. She looked out of the tent, saw Kai, and moved out into the moonlight. It was waning and did not offer much illumination, so Kai nodded his head back towards the fire. Akemi smiled and followed without question.

When they had both seated themselves, Akemi spoke first, "You worry about how much Ienobu thinks of me."

"Yes," Kai answered.

"I know that you all are in danger. The Shogun is a madman with armies and trained killers at his disposal," she added. Kai took the cue to just let her speak her piece and only nodded to agree. "I do not wish Ienobu any harm. I know that he is in enough trouble simply for speaking on my behalf. I am not going to try to talk him out of whatever you all are planning."

Kai paused a moment and smiled. He almost wished that he could send her back to her grandfather in Hagi. Whatever was in store for her at Edo, ease and peace were not likely in store. "Akemi, do you love Ienobu?" he asked. She turned her head away from Kai, but he could tell even in the low light that she was blushing.

"I believe I do, but I have never been in love before," she said quietly.

"Do you understand that you will never be able to be with him? I do not enjoy the role that I have to play here, but I believe that someone needs to be the speaker of truth in this situation. You are right to call the Shogun a madman, but I think you put too much trust in Ienobu's words. He cannot protect you from his father. It would be best if you left the processional in the next city. Sensei or I can pay someone to escort you home, you and your grandfather can move further south, and that will likely be the end of the entire situation," Kai offered.

"No. That just will not do," Akemi added shaking her head. "I am here for a reason. God has allowed me to have the ear of the next Shogun, and when he rules, he will remove the restrictions on my faith. He has already promised me. Ienobu believes deeply, but broadly. He finds virtue in many paths, and he sees no reason that my path should be forbidden."

"But he is not Shogun now, and there are perhaps many years before he will take that title. How are you willing to take the chance that Iemitsu will not stomp out your religion out of pure spite?" Kai asked.

Akemi looked at Kai for a long time before she answered. "Kai, where do you place your faith?" she asked.

It was a question that Kai asked himself more and more often these days. "It is hard for me to trust what I cannot predict and what I cannot understand. I trust my skill with a katana. I trust the teachings of my father and my sensei. And I trust in the goodness in Ienobu's heart. Beyond that, I cannot truly say," he answered honestly.

"I trust in the Lord, and in the power of his might," Akemi said. She stood, and Kai walked her back to her tent. By the time he made it back to his tent, the conversation had run itself through his head several times. Kai understood that he had made no headway toward his goal, and decided to retire for the night. He would wait for whatever the morning brought him.

***

The morning brought much of the same, as did the next and those after. They had reached an impasse. All agreed that Hotta was dangerous and that he must be removed; however, none was able to predict how Iemitsu would respond to claims against his favorite general. Kai once again brought up the prospect of trying to bring Masako into the conspiracy. So strong was the impression she left on him that it took the full weight of both Razan and Ienobu in unison to remove her fully from the equation. Masako played her own game, and she had her own goals. Reluctantly, Kai agreed to drop the argument.

The three eventually decided that the most damaging charge that they could bring against Hotta was that of gross insubordination, against the Shogun himself of course. Even Ienobu doubted his father would care much, if at all, about Hotta's conduct towards the prince. The conspirators planned what they could and hoped for the best.

The night before they arrived back into Edo, the group had a long talk that went well into the early hours. Kai noticed that Ienobu was visibly uncomfortable, but he no longer doubted the young man's resolve. Akemi sat very close to Ienobu, holding his hand. Her presence at a conspiracy talk was strange, yet Ienobu seemed to gain strength from it. At a point, Kai recognized that everyone had gone silent. Each knew his role in what was to come, and eventually, no further words were needed. "I think I am going to try and sleep," Razan announced, breaking the silence. The older man stood slowly, stretching legs that had been bent for many hours, and walked away toward his tent. Kai stood as well and noticed Akemi squeeze Ienobu's hand.

"Good night to you both," Kai said. As he was walking away, he heard Akemi speaking softly yet firmly to Ienobu. He was ten paces from the fire when he heard Ienobu call his name. Kai paused and turned. He saw Akemi sneak a quick kiss on Ienobu's cheek, and then she left.

"Can we... walk a bit under the trees?" Ienobu asked

approaching Kai. Kai nodded and followed the prince out into the forest. The moon was new, and the night was dark, though the patchy foliage of the maple and pine trees allowed what starlight there was to shine through unimpeded. The two walked for several minutes in silence. Ienobu clearly wished to discuss something and was having a hard time working up to it.

Kai thought he should begin the conversation with a friendly tone, but before he was able to do so, Ienobu steeled himself and spoke directly, "This is the last night we will have before we get back into the city so I cannot wait any longer to say this. And, I do not think Akemi would forgive me if I did not." Kai sensed the gravity of the situation and decided it best to allow Ienobu to speak when he was ready. The prince took a deep breath and looked Kai directly in the eyes. Kai saw again, or maybe this was the first pure instance, the ruler that Ienobu would be.

"You killed my uncle in cold blood," Ienobu said.

Kai had not expected the prince to revisit the matter of Tadanaga, but a moment later, he realized how foolish it was to think that way. Just because his actions were necessary for him did not mean that Ienobu understood it. Kai had suffered from the act, genuinely so, yet his purpose in life had been set. He was a living instrument of revenge, and nothing more. Or was he? All of the conflict that he had compacted into the back of his mind suddenly flooded out. He realized that he was crying. "I did," he said weakly.

"You hate my father, and you will take whatever steps you deem needed to have your revenge against him," Ienobu pressed.

"I do, and I will," Kai responded.

"I will never forgive you in this world or the next. I know all of what you are capable. I have seen you murder. I have seen you lie. I have seen you torture a man until his will to live is ground down under your heel. So make no mistake, though I have come to rely on you, you will never take my uncle's place. I will never love you, and I will never consider you my family. We are not equals. You are a nameless orphan, and I am soon to be the Shogun of all of Nihon. Do not believe for another moment that I am unaware," the prince said in astonishing earnestness. Kai was leveled.

He tried to speak, but Ienobu held up a hand to stop him. "I had to tell you that. You needed to understand how I feel. All of what I have said is true, and to that, I will add one further truth. I must be able to trust that you pose no threat to me or this plan has no hope of success." Kai felt stripped to the bone. He found himself kneeling, half out of respect, half because his legs would no longer hold him.

"I do not believe that your death is required for my vengeance to be wrought in full," Kai stated.

"That has not always been true," Ienobu said. It was not a question. "But I believe that is true now. I have my own plans for my father, and I will do my best to keep out of your way. I have no doubts that your plans coincide far enough along the road with mine. It is customary for shoguns to step down into retirement, and I have no problem with my father spending his in abject discomfort."

Ienobu left before Kai could continue the discussion. He was not sure he had anything left to say if the prince had stayed.

***

The next morning, the procession broke camp reasonably late. Edo was only a few hours ride away, and the plans stood to arrive just before the evening meal. They had traveled close to an hour when a rider came thundering up the road behind them. The man was dressed in Tokugawa armor and colors, and Kai recognized his face from Hotta's personal bodyguard. He made no sign of stopping or even slowing until Ienobu shouted for him to stop in the name of the Shogun. The man reluctantly pulled up on the reins and waited for Ienobu's horse to catch up.

"What is your errand?" Ienobu demanded.

"My lord, I carry news to your father from the Nagato Province," the rider spoke quickly.

"Speak on, then," Ienobu said. The rider observed Ienobu's countenance and decided not to push his orders into a breach of conduct. He did seem uncomfortable speaking openly in front of the Kaishakunin, but forms must be kept.

"The lord Hotta Masamori has been seriously injured and even now may be dead," he reported.

"How did this happen? Tell the full tale," the prince responded. Kai was impressed that the young man had kept his tone so even. Kai had almost fallen out of his saddle.

"The lord Hotta was quite... upset when he was left behind. He took it upon himself to conduct... investigations into the attack on your life. The lord Mori Hidenari expressed much concern and told of strong resistance against the Tokugawa regime within certain areas of Hagi, but the lord Hotta would hear none of it. He took us into the city far too late into the night, and we were attacked after interrogating several... suspects," the messenger clearly knew more than he was supposed to let on. Kai doubted that he had shared his whole message either.

"You will travel with us to Edo. We will report our trip in full to my father," Ienobu said. The messenger clearly did not believe that suggestion was in line with his charge.

"My lord, I was instructed to make as much haste as possible. I have slept only as much as I have needed to stay mounted, and I have eaten very little. If you would, please release me to carry on to Edo," the rider explained in a tone that verged on condescension. Kai sensed that the man was hiding something. Ienobu either felt the same.

"You may hold your task completed, and I commend you on your duty. You may be present to recount your story to my father when we meet with him, and I will make certain that you are properly rewarded for your service to my family. You may ride in my party as an honor. Take what refreshment you may. We will be in Edo before sundown," the prince replied.

The rider, trying desperately to hide his disapproval, moved his horse into line several ranks back from Kai and Razan. Ienobu paced his horse so that he ended up between the two. "This has ruined everything," the prince hissed.

"We will make do with what we can," Razan said optimistically, "we still have a few hours to adjust." Kai was not so sure. If Hotta was dead, even the most detailed plan would not be able to predict how Iemitsu reacted. He might quietly withdraw into early retirement and allow his son to rule. The military followed Iemitsu because of his Clan, but they fought for Hotta. Iemitsu surely recognized that fact. Losing that would be a blow to Iemitsu, not to mention the loss of his personal relationship with Hotta. Of course, he might be just as likely to rally the army behind him to wipe out the population of Hagi. Either way, Kai doubted that Iemitsu would be interested in his presence as an adviser. It would be impossible for Kai to make himself invaluable to the Shogun if he were not able to speak with him.

Kai found himself in the very uncomfortable position of hoping with all his heart that Hotta was not dead. Not dead yet, that was.

Chapter 10

"When one's own attitude on courage is fixed in his heart, and when his resolution is devoid of doubt, then when the time comes he will of necessity be able to choose the right move."

- Yamamoto Tsunetomo

The knot of concern in Kai's gut was as large as a nashi pear by the time the procession rode into the palace gates. He could see a small figure dressed in light blue robes standing atop the front stairs of the palace itself. He knew intellectually that it must be Iemitsu, but for a moment he allowed himself to daydream. Kai imagined Kikkawa Hidoyoshi, the most honorable man Kai had ever known, standing at the top of those steps greeting Kikkawa Kai home from a successful diplomatic journey? He shook his head, and the image disappeared. "Now is not the time," he scolded himself out loud.

"It is the only time we have," Razan replied. Kai looked over to his sensei, but Razan clearly understood more of what Kai had thought than anyone else might have. The older man always seemed to know, but Kai allowed himself to stop feeling as if his mind had been invaded. Razan had seen three shoguns come to power and had survived all of them, a feat in itself. His sensei simply knew humanity better than humans knew themselves.

"We are being purified," Ienobu said jutting his chin to point. Kai looked over to the side of the road just inside the gate and saw several conical mounds of sand. "The salt on the morizuna there adds an air of purification to the symbol of hospitality. My father must be in one of his moods again." The prince had explained his father's somewhat fickle relationship with the divine in hopes of securing the best possible outcome for Akemi. Iemitsu tended to believe in only what benefitted him. Everything else was discounted as a misinterpretation caused by the ignorance of the other party. Yet, when the Shogun was convinced of some sign or portent, he could

99

become irrationally attached to it.

As the procession neared the Honmaru, Ienobu's personal retinue broke away. The prince, Hotta's messenger, Akemi, Razan, and Kai crossed over the short earthwork bridge. The stone walls and moat of the castle promised to keep out foes of the Shogun, but here were three walking into the front gate. At the foot of the slowly climbing stairs, the four bowed. Ienobu alone rose to move closer. "And where is Masamori?" Iemitsu asked, "Is he plotting something special?"

"My lord, we should enter the castle and give a full account of our travel," Ienobu deflected. A very tense moment dragged out before the Shogun spun and began to walk back towards the residence. At the top of the stairs, he turned to look at the group.

"Well? Come on!" the Shogun said, clearly irritated. When only Razan, Ienobu, and the bodyguard came to his summons, Iemitsu added, "No, we better have the lot of you. But no weapons." Akemi looked to Kai who nodded in an attempt to assuage any of her fears. They quietly climbed up to meet the rest of the group.

***

Kai never forgot the intensity of the following hours. The Shogun was clearly more perceptive than Kai had allowed, even though Razan warned of just that fact many times over the last weeks. Iemitsu sat and took in the tale, allowing not even a single detail to be omitted. When Ienobu reached the duel between Kai and the Aoki swordmaster, he betrayed a higher opinion of Kai than the Shogun expected. "So, you feel that Masamori's actions were unjust? Do you not see how the Kaishakunin disrespected the leader of my army? Iemitsu asked.

Razan made to interject to support Ienobu, but the prince cut him off with a glare. "You were the one who commanded that the Kaishakunin be returned alive, my lord. And Masamori never forbade Kai from killing his opponent in the duel. Masamori only wished to see Kai dead in such a way that he could circumvent your command. If Kai died defending Tokugawa honor, how could you express anger? Do you not see how the leader of your army disrespected you?" the prince answered his father. Iemitsu looked flabbergasted. Kai wondered how much of the Shogun's response was due to the manner in which his son spoke and how much, if any, doubt might have been created by the question.

As Ienobu went on to describe how savagely Hotta had beaten Kai, the Shogun seemed not to believe his ears, "Is this true?" Iemitsu asked the soldier. The man broke into an immediate attempt to erase any negative stigma of Hotta's actions, but the Shogun slammed his hand down on the low table in front of him. "Speak no more! Nod your head! Did Masamori intend to beat the Kaishakunin to death?!" he bellowed. The soldier froze as if he were afraid that even an involuntary motion might betray his lord. Then, under the intensifying scrutiny of the Shogun, the man nodded his assent.

Kai felt like he had successfully struck a blow against an invincible opponent. Ienobu continued to recount the journey, but Iemitsu seemed only partially interested. He abruptly cut into the story just before Ienobu was reaching the events in Hagi. "Where is Hotta now? I will hear nothing else," he said quietly but firmly enough that all understood the command.

Ienobu ceded the floor to the bodyguard. The man's face had gone an ashen grey at the thought that he might have been the agent of doom for his lord Hotta. "My lord Tokugawa, when I last saw the lord Hotta, he lay near death on the deck of a ship in Hagi port," he reported weakly.

At this news, Iemitsu shot up to his feet, his face moving from deep thought to outright panic. "WHAT?!" he yelled. The others in the room quickly bowed in submission. The Shogun took a moment to compose himself, then after he failed to do so, he left the room. Ienobu ventured a gaze back at Razan who only shrugged from his kneeling position. All knew that the next few moments would be crucial to not only their plot but their survival. Only Ienobu stood a higher than likely chance of making it out alive, and that was due more to the Shogun's personal disgust towards participating in actions that would produce heirs than to any emotional attachment to his son. When the Shogun returned to the room, Kai noticed that his face was red and his eyes puffy.

"How did Masamori come to be near death?" he asked shakily. If the bodyguard were allowed to speak first, he would shape the story to Hotta's benefit. Ienobu broke in quickly in an attempt to gain back whatever ground the conspirators had gained.

"I commanded that he stay behind for a week..." the prince

attempted.

"You commanded?!" Iemitsu cut him off. "Who are you to command my general?!"

"There was an attempt on my life!" Ienobu pivoted. Kai was not so sure that the prince should have chosen that angle, but he knew better than to say anything. The fact that the Shogun had even allowed Kai into the room was somewhat surprising.

"And Masamori saved you? Was that how he was wounded? Did you command him to stay to save up his strength?" Iemitsu pressed.

"No, the lord Hotta was wounded after we left," Ienobu said and immediately regretted. The Shogun's face contorted through several emotions before settling on one of pure but controlled, rage.

Turning to the bodyguard, the Shogun growled, "Were you present when Masamori was wounded? Did you see it with your own eyes?"

"Yes, my lord," the man replied.

"Tell me how," Iemitsu demanded.

In the next few moments, Kai listened as their carefully laid plans fell to pieces. Not only did the bodyguard put the blame directly on the Kirishitan in Hagi, but he was also apparently more cunning than his demeanor betrayed. In what likely proved to be the damning point, the guard alluded that Ienobu had known how dangerous the city was. Was the prince not at the same dinner when the lord Mori warned of anti-Tokugawa sentiment? By leaving the lord Hotta with only his personal bodyguard, the prince might have been, indirectly of course, responsible for Hotta's current condition. After all, the lord Hotta was merely attempting to investigate the attack on the prince's life. Was it also not worth noting that a Kirishitan was at the scene of the assassination attempt, even the same one that sat in the room with them?

Iemitsu shot such a withering gaze at Akemi that Kai worried she might cry out in fear and try to escape. To her credit, the young woman met his gaze with one of her own. She did not look away even after she moved well into the realm of insubordination. When Ienobu reached out and took her hand, his father roared at him, "NO!"

Ienobu turned to look at his father with such an air of incredulity that Kai actually became worried for the life of the prince. When Iemisu met his son's gaze, the look of rage on the Shogun's face slowly shifted into icy contempt. When he motioned for the messenger to continue with the report, Kai waited for a break in the tension that never came. His wrath was put off but had not subsided.

Iemitsu seemed barely able to control himself. Whether it was due to Hotta's situation, Akemi's bravery, or his son's contempt, Kai could not guess. All he knew was that the Shogun had cracked somehow. His hands clenched into fists and released repeatedly. Flecks of spittle flew from his mouth when he spoke. At several instances in the story, his body visibly shook to the point that his carefully pulled and oiled topknot loosened so that strands of his hair fell down into his face. Kai began to mentally make peace with himself. He honestly believed Iemitsu would kill him, and once death was inevitable, he would do his absolute best to bring the Shogun with him.

Eventually, though, Iemitsu sat back down. For almost an hour, the room was silent. Kai did not even risk looking anywhere other than the floor just in front of him. More than once, he thought of rushing towards Iemitsu, leaping over the table intended to hold the welcome-back meal, and strangling the Shogun with his bare hands. None of them were armed, but Kai was sure he could make due.

"I cannot believe that my own son has cost me the most decorated officer in my entire military. And for what? The love of a Kirishitan?" Iemitsu asked in a surprisingly calm tone. Kai almost wished that the Shogun had continued to scream. The stillness of his voice was even more unsettling.

"My lord, we are not certain of the lord Masamori's death," Razan ventured.

"You know so much less than you appear, Hayashi Razan," Iemitsu answered. "I fell into an ague two days after the sankin-kotai lords left. No doctor in all of Edo was able to treat me. I lay in bed with a pain in my chest, sweating but chilled to the bone. I feared for the safety of those traveling, especially for Hotta. One night several weeks ago, Gongen-sama came to me in a dream. He stretched out his hand and cleansed me with fire." The Shogun paused as if he were conjuring a memory just out of his reach. Clearly, though, Iemitsu believed everything he was saying.

He continued suddenly, "Then, my grandfather showed me another vision. I saw in my hand a katana, perfect in craftsmanship, but to my surprise, it was broken. It fell to the ground in a thousand pieces. I toiled against all the odds to collect each and every piece, and I brought them to Gongen-sama. He approved of my diligence and used his fire to put the pieces back together. However, the strength of the blade would never return. I knew that if it were wielded in battle, it would shatter into a million pieces beyond any repair. Gongen-sama gestured to a stand that held his katana. I understood, and I put my restored katana on the kake next to his.

"I asked my ancestor what I was to wield against my enemies, and he pointed to the kake again. Instead of two blades, I then saw three. The new katana appeared poorly made and had no distinguishing marks. Yet, when I drew it, I saw that it had a cutting edge more keen than any I had ever beheld. When I awoke, I was healed of my malady, but I feared even more. Do you understand, Wise One?" The tone Iemitsu used at "Wise One" clearly meant to belittle Razan.

"No, my lord. Please teach me," Razan humbly answered.

"If I am able to put the pieces of this broken blade back together, Tokugawa Ieyasu will heal Masamori. Gongen-sama will only reward me if I do the hard work to rectify this catastrophe," Iemitsu explained as if he were talking to a child. He stood, "I am weary, but there is work yet to be done this night. Follow me."

All of those in the room stood and followed the Shogun into the courtyard of the Honmaru. The imposing height of the donjon tower was visible even in the gloom of the night. Kai was not comforted by the security it offered. He was already too close to his enemy for retreat, no matter how strong the holdfast. Along the way, Iemitsu commanded several of the household guards to follow as well. Thick clouds hid the moon, so Iemitsu commanded the soldiers to bring lanterns and torches. Upon their return, the group standing in the yard appeared almost ghoulish in the dancing light.

Iemitsu spoke to one of the guards who surrendered his daisho. The Shogun took one of the pairs of blades, the smaller wakizashi, and handed it to Hotta's bodyguard. "You will now commit seppuku to express your shame in allowing your lord Hotta Masamori to be wounded by street rats. You also failed to report directly to me as you were commanded. If you do so, I will hold your death as payment for your shame and forgive you," he said. The guard, who had seemed so proud in his report's ability to sway Iemitsu, only nodded and began to strip off his armor. Iemitsu handed the katana to Kai and added, "You will perform your duty."

Kai's stomach roiled for the hundredth time that night. How easy would it be to take the katana and strike the Shogun down? His hatred for Iemitsu grew again, surprising Kai at the new depths of loathing he discovered. Yet he also realized how much Razan's teachings had changed him. He no longer wished only for Iemitsu's death. Death was too quick of a punishment for such a man. Only years of slow torture full of constant reminders of his failures would come close to footing the bill. The Kaishakunin took the katana and did his duty, quickly and efficiently as ever.

Iemitsu looked down at the corpse and spat into the growing pool of blood at his feet. "You are forgiven," he said. To two of the soldiers, he directed, "Dispose of this coward and let his family know what transpired here. Make certain that they know the depths of my disgust before even breathing a word of the smallest hint of my magnanimous redress. I wish them to know that I am gracious, but only just so." The soldiers nodded and made their way to remove the body and head.

"One piece of the blade collected," Iemitsu stated. Looking back at Kai, he continued, "now kill the Kirishitan."

Chapter 11

"People with intelligence will use it to fashion things both true and false and will try to push through whatever they want with their clever reasoning. This is injury from intelligence."
— *Yamamoto Tsunetomo*

Kai had hardly slept since that night in the courtyard. The ghosts of his past had begun to visit him in his dreams. First, his father and brothers appeared. They stood silently weeping. Kai knew that they mourned because they had failed to teach Kai humility, and for that, he had killed them. Then Tadanaga. He arrived with a hearty laugh, but when he saw Kai, he also began to weep. He wept because he had failed to teach Kai loyalty. Then the Aoki swordmaster, who wept because he had been unable to teach Kai honor. The shinobi cried because they failed to teach Kai how to conceal his motives. Hotta's bodyguard wept because he failed to teach Kai how to navigate a changing landscape. Akemi appeared last, but she did not weep. Her eyes bored into Kai's soul and laid it bare. And once Kai faced all of his failures, blood spilled out of her mouth. So much blood.

He jerked awake with a motion to where his katana would be, but it was not there. It had not been there for some time. The Shogun had moved Kai to a different room inside the castle instead of the more familiar room he had before, tucked in the corner of the Honmaru wall. Kai accepted gratefully, in part because refusing Iemitsu's offer would be seen as an insult. He was also glad that he would have natural light. The new room had a window. His katana, however, was currently held in what Iemitsu called, "safe keeping."

Kai stood and walked to the window of his room. It looked out over the moat and then on to the city. The room was on the second floor of the building, and the moat was another fifteen feet down to account for the stone wall below the base of the building. Kai did not think that he could survive the jump, and he knew that thought had not escaped the Shogun.

Despite what appeared to be a new level of trust from Iemitsu, Kai knew his life was in danger. In one of the few meetings Razan had managed, his sensei related the razor's edge upon which Kai's life was balanced. Iemitsu firmly believed that he might be forced to sacrifice Kai's life to save Hotta's. The Shogun seemed, to Razan, to be maniacally devoted to his interpretation of his dream of Ieyasu, and no amount of reasoning seemed to change his mind. If Hotta arrived from Hagi still close to death, Kai expected to be dead within the hour.

He surveyed the city lights in the distance. He wondered how quickly he could blend into the people. He did not think his face was so well known by the inhabitants of Edo. He suspected that the only reason most people recognized him outside the castle was his proximity to prominent Tokugawa lords. Who else but the Kaishakunin wore the clothes of a peasant and rode in the retinue of the prince? For a moment, Kai longed to attempt the jump down into the moat. It would be a decent sprint through the winding paths down the hill, then across the parade yard, another climb over the main castle wall, down into the main moat, and then he would be free into the city. On second thought, perhaps it would not be as easy as it sounded in his head. Besides, what would he do if he managed to get out of the castle? He knew enough about manual labor to find work at an inn. He could save enough to travel south, back home. But what was left for him there? Nothing. And why was that? Tokugawa Iemitsu.

The acid burn in his chest flared and refused to subside. What good was running away when Iemitsu would go on unpunished? But what else was there to do? Kai was not allowed out of the room, and even if he did get out, he would run into Iemitsu's new pets. During the trip to the south, Iemitsu had called up a firearms specialist and trained an entire squad of ashigaru to use tanegashima muskets. Nobunaga had used the guns in his wars, and somehow, they had made their way into the hands of Iemitsu who knew precisely how he wanted to use them. At this point, there were nearly a dozen ashigaru armed with bedeviled tanegashima either just outside his door or on rooftops nearby. Kai had never even held one of the contraptions and had only conceptual ideas on how to defeat someone wielding one. The odds were definitely not in his favor. He craved information from the outside, but little to nothing made it to his ears. He had only seen Razan a handful of times and had not seen Ienobu at all.

His heart broke again when he thought of the prince. That night under the clouds, Kai had not been able to see Ienobu very well, but Kai knew that Akemi's death hurt Ienobu deeply. Through the flickering torchlight, Ienobu's gaze met Kai's for a brief moment, yet in that moment Kai was overwhelmed by the depths of sadness he perceived. The prince did not cry out to his father to reverse his decision. He understood just as Kai and Razan did that an Iemitsu was in a dangerous mood. If they strayed even a hair's breadth, their plan would fall to ruin. Ienobu knew that even if Kai had turned the blade against the Shogun then and there, none of the conspirators would have survived. There were too many guards, and neither Ienobu nor Razan was armed. Even if Kai were able to take five guards before they responded, ten more stood ready to protect their lord. So, Ienobu silently watched, betraying not even the slightest attachment to Akemi.

The young woman astonished Kai by forgiving him just before he struck. She claimed to know her destination and accepted her death without remorse. If Iemitsu had not barked at Kai to hurry to the task, Kai doubted he would have had the heart to follow through. And so, Kai was haunted. The dead in his wake increased, and Kai felt no closer to sating his revenge.

Kai watched as the sun peeked out over the horizon. Another night marked with only a few hours of sleep. His eyes fought to gain focus in the new light, and he reached up to wipe away the sleepiness. He only managed to make his eyes feel fuzzy instead of heavy. With a defeated sigh, he decided that it was time to begin again. He would take what he had and find a way to make it work. He sat facing the window and breathed a few deep breaths to still himself. He was interrupted immediately by the door opening behind him. Kai sighed again, this time out of frustration. Was he unable to complete even the simplest of tasks? Kai turned to see Hotta Jubei standing in the door. He had not seen Jubei in many months, since the night at Tadanaga's party. The Shogun had sent the wakadoshiyori into the north to spy on the daimyo there. Kai wondered if he could get the man to draw his katana. After all, he had bested Jubei from the very beginning. That must sting the man's pride. This might be just the break Kai needed.

"What brings you back to Edo?" Kai asked with too much of an edge. Jubei tensed as if he wanted to attack Kai on the spot, but he willed himself to calm within a moment.

"As soon as I heard of my brother's situation, I returned to offer my services to the Shogun," Jubei explained through gritted teeth.

"Hoping to take dear Hotta's spot if he died?" Kai supplied. At that, Jubei was not able to contain himself. He lashed out a kick that would have hit Kai in the head, but Kai rolled out of the way. He came up ready to receive more blows, but Jubei restrained himself. The two men stood for several heartbeats before Jubei scoffed at Kai.

"The lord Tokugawa demands your presence," he said. Kai decided that Jubei must have been told to avoid violence. Kai walked out of his room to find ashigaru on either side of the door holding tanegashima ready to fire. He let out a chuckle at his own expense. It would have done no good to disarm Jubei anyway. As soon as he stepped out of the door, he would have been gunned down.

Jubei filed out of the room behind him and shoved Kai down the right end of the hallway. The ashigaru followed just behind Jubei, a constant threat against any escape attempt. After ten minutes of passages and turns, Jubei led Kai into the presence of the Shogun. Iemitsu was reclining on a cushion eating his morning meal. Surprisingly, to his right sat Ienobu. Kai looked to the prince who met his gaze. Kai had never before seen anger mixed with such sadness. The food before the prince was untouched, and the young man appeared to have slept as little as Kai. Kai knew better than to try to communicate. Instead, he allowed Jubei to push him down into a kneeling position before Iemitsu.

"Greetings, Kaishakunin," Iemitsu said between bites. "Have you broken your fast yet?"

Kai reined in the disgust in his voice before he answered, "No, my lord." The Shogun motioned, and within moments, a servant returned with a tray of food for Kai. On it was a small bowl of rice, a raw egg, and some natto.

"I like to mix the egg and soybeans with the rice like this," Iemitsu said tilting his bowl down so that Kai could view its contents. "Try it." Kai could not doubt his hunger. He cracked the egg one-handed, which brought a chuckle of delight from the Shogun, and added the fermented natto to the mix. Using a spoon, he brought up a bite to his mouth, but he stopped short of eating. The pause was not missed. "Come now, do you think that I would poison you?" Iemitsu asked. "If I wanted you dead, you would be." The reasoning was sound, and Kai took the bite. To his surprise, the mixture was actually quite good.

The Shogun and Kai ate quietly for a few minutes. Kai had not recognized how much he missed the taste of anything other than rice, and he finished his meal quickly. Once they were both finished, Iemitsu motioned again, and the servants removed the food trays. Ienobu's meal remained untouched.

"Now, we can speak properly," Iemitsu said. "I have been informed that Masamori's ship will arrive in port today. I have no word on his wellbeing, other than the fact that he still lives. I want you to understand what will happen so that you understand your role in the future. Gongen-sama revealed to me that he would heal Masamori if I toiled to hold those who caused his suffering responsible for their actions. I must gather up the pieces of the broken sword, remember? To that end, his entire bodyguard has committed seppuku, and the Kirishitan in Hagi have been sufficiently punished. You played a part in this reckoning such as it were. I cannot continue to risk Masamori's life in such reckless errantry, so if he survives, he will be promoted to head the entire wakadoshiyori. At that point, I will need a new captain for my palace guard. Assuming you had nothing to do with the attack in Hagi, you will be the honed but unadorned blade from my dream.

"I will question Masamori directly about the events in the south. I do not doubt that he will warn me about your loyalty, but I admit that I cannot find fault with you of late. According to Hayashi Razan and my son, you acted honorably and nobly in all ways, and my dream seems to exonerate you as well. However, if Masamori is... dead," at that Iemitsu waivered, "or he cannot give an account, I will see that as a sign that my task of collecting pieces is not yet complete. You will die, and if that does not bring Masamori back, all the soldiers on the trip will die. I will spare none but my own heir to return Masamori to health. And had I another son..." he said with a nauseated look, "Ienobu would be forfeit as well."

At that confession, Ienobu recoiled in anger, "Do you truly value the life of a retainer more than the life of your son?" Iemitsu's composure, which had to that point seemed very casual to Kai, shattered into fury.

"I value you less than the servants who brought me my food! Your only purpose is to continue the name of Tokugawa once I die, and woe betide our family name once you take over the bakufu. None of the generals respect you, and I doubt that any would follow your edicts!" Iemitsu spat like poison.

Ienobu shot back, "Then send me to the north to be with my mother! I will live out the rest of your years so far away as to be no bother to you!"

The Shogun let out an unexpected, throaty laugh. "You fool! Your mother is dead! I killed her with my own hands moments after she pushed you out!" Iemitsu roared.

"You said she was sent to the north to live in a monastery!" Ienobu cried out.

"I never said such a thing. That lie was dreamed up by my dear brother to make you feel better when you cried!" Iemitsu said breaking into sarcastic laughter. Ienobu stormed out of the room in a rage. Kai was at a loss as to what he should do. He knew better than to simply follow Ienobu, one did not leave the presence of the Shogun without permission. So, Kai sat still. Iemitsu went on chuckling to himself for a few moments before finally sighing in contentment. "If I did not know it to be a fact, I would claim that boy has not a single drop of Tokugawa blood in his body," he said.

Iemitsu looked to Kai, who did his best to hide all emotion from his face. "Go make ready. Hotta's ship should be here in just a few hours. I would have you there, just in case," Iemitsu said returning to his previous, casual, demeanor.

As Jubei led Kai back to his room, or cell as it may be, Kai tried to wrap his head around the situation. It seemed both fitting and ridiculous that Kai's life would soon be determined by how a lunatic interpreted a dream. It had always been the plan to remove Hotta in favor of Kai, but he had never expected Hotta to live through it.

A moment later, Kai heard the ashigaru outside speaking low. He could not ascertain their topic. Clearly, there was some kind of disagreement between two sides. One side finally won out, and it was quiet again. Kai returned to his seated position in front of the window, took another deep breath, and began to try to move the pieces around to make a different picture. He decided to focus specifically on what he knew about the docks of the city, which was not much, and ways to make himself less easy to hit with a bullet. That point, at least, could not be terribly different from an arrow, save that the bullet moved much faster. He knew to prepare for the worst and was well into it when the door opened without even a knock.

Kai turned, expecting it to be a summoning messenger that Hotta's ship had arrived early. Instead, it was Masako. She was dressed as a servant, but there was no mistaking the intensity of her eyes. "When we last spoke, you told me that you did not want to see Ienobu dead. But it turns out that you had seriously considered it for some time, only before being brought to your senses just days ago. Then, you almost got him killed!" she rasped somewhere just above the range of a whisper. "What did you think would happen with both you and Razan pushing him into the seat of power so early?! Razan has already done his best to explain away his guilt, but I would appreciate a straight answer from you," she added.

"It was the only way we saw," Kai answered honestly. She clearly knew the whole plot already. There was no sense obfuscating.

"Well, that only proves that you are either near-sighted or blind. Ienobu is in pieces. He is so far from being able to lead that it is no longer an option. You and Razan have stepped in manure and cannot even smell it. If only all men were as dense as the two of you, I would not have so much trouble getting what I want," Masako complained.

Kai could not doubt that Masako was an imposing figure, and he knew to be wary around her, but to that point, he had never really understood why. Risking her anger, he decided to interject. "My Lady, it might be that if you would let someone else in on your plans, he might offer help instead of causing trouble. In fact, I see nothing to the credit of your plan except being able to change the guard outside my room and sneak in disguised as a commoner," he commented.

"You cannot see my plan because it is a good one!" she spat back at him. "I live days away in Kyoto, but I still know everything that happens in this city. I know what my brother has for breakfast because the cook owes the wellbeing of his mother to me. I know who speaks with my brother and on what topics because his door warden's sister is ill, and I am paying for her treatment. I was the reason Ienobu was sent on the sankin-kotai journey because Date

Masamune owed me a favor and made the suggestion to my brother. Once you and Razan decided to tag along, I was the one who made sure Hotta was able to contact the group of shinobi that attacked you. You do not see me, because I do not wish to be seen!"

Kai worked his mouth to try to make words, but he found none for some time. "If you have something to say, spit it out. We do not have much time," Masako said. Kai thought it was the nicest thing she had ever said to him.

"You put Hotta in contact with the shinobi who almost killed me?" Kai finally managed.

"They worked for me in the first place. Why do you think they were only using paralyzing poison and not puffer fish extract? I wanted there to be a fight. I instructed them to wait until you and Ienobu were alone, or at least alone enough. They knew that they were facing a worthy opponent, and I would win either way. If they killed you, you would finally be out of my hair, and I would not have to plan for the whirlwind of confusion that you add to every situation. If you defeated them, Iemitsu would pull you closer. What I did not count on was Ienobu being thrust into the middle of it so quickly. You should have forbidden him to speak with the Kirishitan," Masako explained.

"I tried to send her away, but she was called by her god to stay by his side. You are right though that he found his courage because of her," Kai stated.

"Of course I am right! And you forget that he has now lost his nerve because of her!" she retorted. She sighed, exasperated from having to explain herself to an inferior. "You are now part of my plan," she said. "You have one job, and I will not be able to be directly involved. I am, for all purposes, not here at this very moment. Ienobu is the key to all of this. If he is to reign, Iemitsu must retire, and you must assure that this happens. You will do this quietly, and you will do this quickly. I will know everything that you say and do, and if you do not succeed, the shinobi will be shooting to kill. This is not a threat, and you do not have any choice in the matter."

Before Kai could rejoin, Masako threw open the door and disappeared into the hired help.

***

Iemitsu had the docks and road back to the palace lined by loyal Tokugawa soldiers in preparation for Hotta's return. Others were erecting a pavilion at the end of the pier by the time Kai arrived under the ever-present threat of tanegashima and Jubei, though only the guns worried Kai. Those and the threat of death from the shogun if Hotta was not alive. And also the new threat of death from Masako. So, three things. But the guns were the most present danger, and Kai decided to focus on them for the moment. There was a speck out on the horizon that must be the ship carrying Hotta, for as soon as the Shogun saw it, he began to pace the length of the pavilion.

The ship's approach lasted over an hour, and Iemitsu seemed more and more uneased the closer it got. Kai had hoped to have a word with Ienobu, but the prince was nowhere to be found. When the gangplank finally thudded down onto the dock, and Hotta Masamori appeared at its head, the Shogun almost cried out with joy. Hotta was unharmed, save that his sword arm was in a sling. He moved almost majestically down the wooden walkway and made his way to Iemitsu. Upon reaching his lord, Hotta dropped to a knee.

"My lord, Tokugawa," he said firmly in a loud voice, "I return to you out of the gaping maw of death." Kai could not keep himself from snorting. At the noise, Jubei cuffed him aside the ear roughly. Iemitsu reached down and pulled Hotta back into a standing position.

"My most loyal and honored servant, I welcome you home with joy and a great reward!" the Shogun cried out loud enough for most of those present to hear. Hotta bowed at the waist. As he raised himself up, he caught sight of Kai.

"Lord, why is that one still alive?" he asked scornfully. Iemitsu looked over to Kai shrugged.

"Your health has proved his innocence. Gongen-sama visited me again in a dream, you see. My grandfather believes that the Kaishakunin is truly loyal to my cause. Once you are promoted, he will take your place," he answered. Kai smiled genuinely. His new station would make it so much easier to deprive Iemitsu the only two things he genuinely cared about. Hotta would die, and then Iemitsu would suddenly decide, at the edge of Kai's katana, to retire to stew in his own misery until the end of his days.

"Lord, the Kaishakunin is at this moment plotting both our deaths. You must reconsider this decision," Hotta hissed.

"Nonsense! We will have the noon meal here on the water to celebrate your safe return. Then, I will hear your story as we walk back to the castle, and I will instruct you where you are wrong. After all, you and I were both healed from the "maw of death" by the power of Gongen-sama. How then can you deny that his message to me is false?" Iemitsu reasoned.

As the Shogun led Hotta over to the table set under the pavilion, Kai noticed Razan slip up the gangplank and onto the ship. He wondered what his sensei was up to, but he tried not to stare in case he aroused attention. Hotta glared at Kai throughout the entire meal and spoke only when the Shogun questioned him. "Don't get in one of your moods!" Iemitsu chided his general. Hotta was not pleased, and when he tried to act otherwise, he did so poorly.

Chapter 12

"Life is not so important when forced to choose between life and integrity."
— *Yamamoto Tsunetomo*

That night, Razan visited Kai in his room. The guard around Kai had been removed again, but Kai suspected that he was still being watched. When Razan silenced Kai with a hand as soon as he entered the room, Kai's suspicion was confirmed. Razan produced a roll of paper, ink, and two pens.

"Both rooms full of ashigaru," he wrote along the edge of the piece of paper. Kai read it, and Razan pointed right and left.

"Shogun scared or Hotta?" Kai wrote back. Razan pointed his pen at Hotta's name. He took back the paper and wrote for several moments.

"Sailors on the boat all say Hotta never hurt. Hotta angry and insulted. Message from the south was a lie to punish prince, get Akemi killed," he wrote. Kai's loathing for Hotta deepened. It was utterly believable that the general would sink to such levels. Ienobu's actions had cost Hotta credibility in the eyes of his troops, and Hotta was not accustomed to being on the receiving end of a scolding.

"Does Ienobu know?" Kai wrote back. Razan nodded once.

"How is he?" Kai continued.

"Devastated. Not eating. Not sleeping. I am worried. Wants to speak with you," Razan scribbled.

"Can he visit?" Kai responded.

"Cannot come here. Sword lesson tomorrow. Must be brief. Hotta suspects everyone." Razan wrote. Kai nodded that he understood. Razan rose and almost ripped the paper, but Kai waived him back down. Razan looked at the door but put the paper back down.

"Masako came to see me." Kai wrote. "Wants me to get Iemitsu to resign. Told me I was dead if I failed."

117

Razan's eyes widened, and he blew out a long breath. "She knows our plan. Ienobu must have told her. She is very dangerous. Tensions are high right now. I did not know she came to Edo. Must have thought it was important," he wrote back. The paper was almost covered with scribbles. Kai turned it over and found a clear corner.

"Advice?" he wrote and then looked at Razan plaintively.

"Be careful. Trust no one other than us," was all his Sensei could offer. He rose again and tore the page into small pieces. He threw them out of the window and left the room. There was much to be considered from the few words they had exchanged. Kai took a moment to silently thank Razan for teaching him how to read and write in the first place.

Kai had not expected Hotta to quietly accept an administrative position. He enjoyed the physicality of violence too much. It was a testament to his intelligence that Hotta had managed to work out the conspiracy, and Kai had to remind himself that disliking an opponent did not make him any less dangerous. What if Hotta's plan to punish Ienobu went further than Akemi? There was already evidence that Hotta still suspected Kai. The guards in the next rooms were testament enough to that.

Kai stared out the window into the night. He suddenly felt very alone. Seeing Ienobu the next day would offer a chance to regain his footing. Yes. Tomorrow. With that thought, Kai fell down onto his bed and slept untroubled for the first time in many nights.

***

The next afternoon, one of the shogun's personal guards came to fetch Kai to the lesson. On the way past the next room, he quickly threw open the door to find three very startled ashigaru. "I will be out for a while if you all need to refresh yourselves," he said with a smile. The men quickly soured, and the one closest to the door slammed it back shut. Kai could not keep from laughing.

When he reached the courtyard, Ienobu was already there moving through practice drills. Kai watched the young man for a moment. He had come a very long way and was well on pace to catch up to samurai of his age. Yet he was ever so much older than his years. "That only works if your opponent is taller than you!" Kai called across the yard. Ienobu looked over, saw Kai, and nodded. He repeated the drill, but at the appointed time, switched to a mid-level swing.

Kai received his katana from the soldier and moved out to meet Ienobu. "I only practice with you, and you are taller than I," Ienobu said, taking a moment to wipe sweat from his forehead. "Shall we spar?" he asked. Kai moved a few paces away from Ienobu and tucked his scabbard into his belt sash. He took the proper position and nodded to Ienobu.

Ienobu appraised the distance to his opponent and settled down into his own stance, balancing his weight on the balls of his feet to respond quickly if Kai attacked first. Ienobu had not initially taken kindly to Kai's instruction to avoid stances designed for powerful blows. The young man had commented that fighting was about striking your opponent down, not dancing around him. That day, Kai danced around Ienobu and swatted the prince in his rear with the flat of his katana for an hour. After that, Ienobu understood the importance of quickness.

"Razan told me you needed to speak," Kai said low enough to not be overheard by the guards around the courtyard, which he noticed were more numerable than they were moments before.

"We will have our window tomorrow. My father is planning a ceremony to promote Masamori," Ienobu said. He drew his blade quickly and attempted to catch Kai with the upstroke of the action. Kai leaned back, watching the tip of Ienobu's katana flash harmlessly by. He took two steps back and resumed his stance.

"How will this work? I am being watched at all hours," Kai responded. His sword swept out widely. He purposefully moved slow enough for Ienobu to parry the blow and step inside his guard. He dropped his left hand down to pull Ienobu's arm, spinning the boy around and to the ground.

As Ienobu accepted Kai's hand to get back up, the prince added, "He also plans to allow you to take the name Kikkawa in the same ceremony." Kai almost dropped Ienobu. Kikkawa Kai? Could it be true? "Again?" Ienobu asked.

Kai nodded, but his mind swam with possibility. He would have the chance to rebuild his family's honor. He would have a name. A clan. He would belong. For so long, he had been an outsider, a man of no honor in a culture that valued honor above all. When Ienobu attacked, the prince had to hold his blow. Kai had not even moved to block.

"Kai!" Ienobu said. He looked up to the prince and put away his thoughts for the moment. "You must pay attention. There is little time, and I must explain how we are to proceed. The plan must change." Over the course of the next hour, Kai grew more and more detached from the world around him. Ienobu detailed how the ceremony was to proceed. He explained his plan and both his and Kai's roles in it. They would act just after Hotta had been promoted. At that time, the Shogun would announce a special surprise, and Ienobu would escort Kai to the dais at the end of the parade ground. Ienobu planned to act before Kai was officially named. There would be no Kikkawa Kai.

"Is there no other way?" Kai asked Ienobu after the prince had explained the plan.

"There is not," Ienobu said sadly. "I no longer have the heart to be what you and Razan wish for me. Not after learning about my mother. Not after Akemi… I know what I am asking you to do, and I know you may regret it until the last of your days. But I see no other way to make my father pay for what he has done."

"If we are to proceed, I must do something first," Kai said. He pulled his scabbard from his belt and returned his blade to it. He reached down and removed the Tokugawa blade from Ienobu's belt. "You have never formally received your sword. But I give you this blade for two reasons. First, no one should ever doubt that you have become a man. Second, it is a pledge of my service to the true lord of the Tokugawa Clan, for I will follow your path to vengeance and make it my own. It will honor me if you wear it tomorrow." Ienobu nodded. Without another word, he turned and left.

Kai tried for the rest of his life to remember anything from that night, but all he could summon was the memory of unnumbered tears.

**

The morning came, and attendants arrived in Kai's room. They bathed him, washed his hair, and dressed him in a fine kimono. On its back was a circle crossed by three reeds, the mon of the Kikkawa Clan. He thought back to the one his father wore when teaching, and for a brief moment allowed himself to pretend that he would be able to follow Hidoyoshi's footsteps. But Kikkawa Kai was a dream that would never come to be. He half expected armor, but none was provided. Neither was he armed. These last two precautions likely came at Hotta's insistence.

Razan came soon after. The two men found that they had little to say. They exchanged greetings, but nothing more. Kai almost allowed his emotions to overwhelm him, but when Razan clapped him on the back, his resolution stiffened. "To the job," Razan said.

The two men walked stoically through the Honmaru and down to the gate. The dizzying array of paths made more sense to Kai then than they had when he first entered the castle, and his feet, though they were heavy, knew the way to the parade ground without much steering from his mind. Kai heard through time his father admonishing his youngest brother, Hidosuke, "Emotion should always be the horse, never the rider. Control your emotions, do not allow them to control you!" Even Hidoyoshi's words could not make his feet feel less like ship anchors. Across the land bridge, over the moat, the parade ground was full to the brim with Tokugawa soldiers. A broad path cut down the middle ending in a large dais that had been erected against the back wall, two-hundred paces away.

"It is a beautiful day," Kai heard. Turning he saw Iemitsu in full armor, black trimmed with dazzling gold, surrounded by retainers flying the hollyhock mon of Tokugawa. As he passed Kai, the Shogun paused. "I have quite the surprise for you," he said with a devilish grin. Kai almost replied the same, but the pit in his stomach had swallowed all of his words.

The Shogun was announced with a shout, and the soldiers in the parade ground snapped to attention. Kai counted each step the Shogun took to the dais and used that to calculate how much time he would have. Not more than thirty seconds, surely. It would be enough. Hotta appeared beside Kai. "I have done all within my power to stop this aberration of form. You are a nameless wastrel, and you have no honor whatsoever. The lord Tokugawa is convinced of your loyalty and is willing to turn the world over for the sake of a fever dream, but I am absolutely not. Do not forget my words, cur," he growled at Kai.

"You will never forget this day," Kai managed with extreme effort. Hotta glared at him but moved out to the end of the path.

When the Shogun climbed the steps, the soldiers spun to face him. It was an impressive display. "My samurai!" Iemitsu shouted, his voice barely carrying to the back. "Today, we gather to honor Hotta Masamori!" At this, a cheer sprang from the men. With the cheer, Hotta began his approach. The soldiers took up the chant of "Hotta! Hotta!" When Hotta reached the dais, he knelt in honor of the Shogun.

"My servant Hotta Masamori! Today, I appoint you to head of my wakadoshiyori! I also increase your yearly allotment by five-thousand koku! In recognition of service to the Tokugawa, I also present to you this katana from Gongen-sama's personal collection! Rise and take this blade!" Iemitsu shouted. Hotta stood and climbed up all but the last two steps. He knew better than to assume equality with Iemitsu. He took the proffered katana, unsheathed it, and held it high for the soldiers to inspect. This brought another cheer from the crowd.

"Are you ready to play your part?" Ienobu said from Kai's side. Kai had not heard him arrive over the roar of the crowd.

"Are you certain thus us the only way?" Kai answered. Ienobu stood as resolute as stone.

"Shall I ask you a second time? Must you be cowed by convention?" Ienobu retorted.

"No. There is no need," Kai said, resigned.

Kai saw the Shogun hold up a hand. At that sign, the crowd silenced. "I have a special announcement! Kaishakunin, join us!" Iemitsu shouted. At this, a great murmur went through the crowd.

Before the two men began walking, Ienobu spoke once more, "I said that I would never love you and that I would never call you family. I also said that I was your better, and I still believe all of those to be true. But know this, I do find honor in you." Before Kai could answer, Ienobu had started down the path. Kai took several quick steps to catch up to the prince.

When the two men were in the middle of the path, Ienobu halted. He pulled open his kimono and dropped to his knees. With every ounce of his strength, he shouted, "Soldiers of the Tokugawa! My father has strayed from the honorable path! He has led the country astray and brought shame on our ancestors! I call you all as witnesses to this act!"

Kai reached down and retrieved his katana from Ienobu's sash where it had been held in safekeeping since the day before. Ienobu produced his own wakizashi, the hollyhock mon flashed in gold on its pommel. Kai heard Iemitsu bellow something from the dais and looked to see Hotta stumbling down the steps towards them in an attempt to stop the inevitable. Kai looked to Ienobu. The prince held his wakizashi to his stomach and looked up to meet Kai's gaze one last time.

"Sir, I have been designated as your assistant. Rest assured, I shall not fail you," Kai said. Ienobu made his cut quickly and without making a noise. Hotta was yelling at the men to stop Ienobu, but to do so would have dishonored the kanshi-seppuku. It was well within Ienobu's rights to take his life in protest of his lord's actions. For what he hoped would be the last time, Kai performed the kaishaku.

Seconds later, Hotta was on him with both katana and wakizashi drawn. Kai batted the blades with a flurry of ripostes that halted Hotta's advance. "You coward!" Hotta bellowed. Space allowed Kai to compose himself. He gave ground to Hotta, moving out towards the back of the parade ground. He needed to get out of the troop formation. Luckily, none of the troops intervened in the duel after Hotta cut the hand off of the first one who tried. "He is mine!" he cried.

Hotta was skilled indeed, but Kai was skill incarnate. Once Kai felt that he would have a chance to end Hotta and make his escape, he took the next opportunity he could to begin his work. Hotta led in with his wakizashi coming low, and Kai knew that dropping his katana to block would trigger Hotta's katana to come across high. Instead, Kai jumped, tucking his legs under him to dodge the thrust. Hotta had expected to use Kai's block to steady himself for the counterattack, and when Kai did not act predictably, Hotta stumbled forward, right into Kai's kick. Hotta took the kick to the head and fumbled his short blade. Kai brought his blade up to finish his opponent when a loud bang echoed across the parade ground.

Kai felt pain explode against his side. He turned his head to see the cloud of powder still dissipating from the end of a tanegashima. Iemitsu was among the ashigaru berating them to kill the traitor. Hotta had recovered and moved purposefully into their line of fire. They would not risk shooting if Hotta could be hit. The bullet had lodged into Kai's side, and a fist-sized patch of blood already soaked through his kimono. He was in no position to fight, and Hotta was in no mind to allow him to leave.

"At last, you will get what is coming to you!" Hotta yelled. Kai found after he blocked the first two blows, that he could generate little power with his right arm. He switched his grip to his left, but he was losing blood. Hotta pressed his advantage, and try as he might, Kai found that he could not focus. As much as it would haunt him, he had to run. Hotta gave a mighty swing across Kai's waist, and when Kai tried to move back to dodge it, he tripped over his own feet.

Hotta laughed in triumph and moved forward, his katana turned to stab Kai and pin him to the ground. In a moment of clarity, Kai grabbed up a handful of dirt. When Hotta took another step, Kai threw it into the man's face. Hotta sputtered, and Kai swung his katana up in an arc to cut between Hotta's chest plate and his leg armor. The blade bit deep, and Hotta collapsed into a heap. Kai scrambled up to his feet and began to run with all he had left. He got to the moat and found Razan waiting disguised as a commoner many years older than he was. Kai half-fell down the five-foot drop into the waiting boat, and Razan immediately began to pole them away. The cracks of tanegashima soon rang out, and bullets whizzed by the boat. In his wisdom, Razan had chosen the short side of the castle wall, and soon he poled the boat around the corner, shielding the pair from the aim of the ashigaru.

***

"Well, my friend, it looks like you succeeded," Razan said as he attended the bullet wound on Kai's side. They had made their way into the city to a house that Razan had prepared. It seemed that many in Edo believed in their cause, only very quietly so.

"If that was a success, I do not wish to know what failure feels like," Kai said despondently.

"Ienobu was a brave man. Perhaps the bravest man that I have ever met. He lived the last year of his life exactly as he wished, and died in the same way. To feel sorry for him diminishes the honor in his actions," Razan admonished. When Kai did not agree, Razan continued, "To feel sorry for yourself does the same." Kai reluctantly accepted the lesson and sat quietly while Razan worked to clean the gunshot wound. The bullet had wedged itself three inches into his gut, though it miraculously had not severely damaged any of his organs. Razan had been forced to use his fingers to probe the wound and extract the bullet. Kai never wished to feel that again. Even the ample amounts of sake he had drunk did little to lessen the discomfort.

"You are lucky," Razan said as he held a linen pad down on Kai's abdomen. He made a motion for Kai to press it, and when he did, Razan found another strip of linen to wrap around Kai's midriff to hold it in place.

"I do not feel lucky, I feel like I was shot," Kai said. The pain radiated out from the wound. It had missed organs, but it had torn the muscle. He was facing many weeks of soreness. What else lay ahead?

"I think that it is time for me to go," Kai said looking at the kimono that he had worn that day. Razan had hung it on the wall to wash the blood out of it.

"Where will you go, Kai?" Razan asked.

"I do not think I should go north," Kai said. He had no idea how Masako would react once she heard what had gone on. It was enough for Kai to know that he had once again ruined her plans. The threat of running into another group of hired assassins was not promising.

"No, I do not think that would be wise at all," Razan said, understanding what had gone unspoken.

"It will be Winter soon," Kai said offhand.

"Even more reason to stay out of the North," Razan added.

Kai looked at his sensei and did not respond for a long time. When he did, he said, "Kikkawa Kai was a figment of my imagination. He died on the parade ground beside Tokugawa Ienobu, the only man he ever considered his lord. Tokugawa Iemitsu still sits in power, but I have learned the limits of one man against an army." He gestured to the wound as proof. "I am not invincible, and I cannot fight him alone. I will go where there are enemies of the Shogun, and I will be nothing more than the Kaishakunin."

Epilogue

"Nothing is impossible in this world. Firm determination, it is said, can move heaven and earth. Things appear far beyond one's power because one cannot set his heart on any arduous project due to want of strong will."
— *Yamamoto Tsunetomo*

Kai trudged up the side of the hill. He had been on the road for weeks, or months, he had lost count. Cresting the top, he looked out over the valley below him. The trees had given up most of their foliage, and like their branches, Kai felt bare. He had been moving steadily southward and had made his way into the mountains. Winter was upon him, and snow had already become a serious threat. Scanning the clouds, one such storm appeared to be catching up to him rather quickly, so he decided to seek shelter for the night.

Crouched in a low cave, Kai tried to start a fire. Nothing around him was dry enough to catch, and it was just as well. He reckoned that he was out of Fudai territory, but drawing attention to himself was probably not the best of ideas anyway. Razan had friends who had smuggled him out of Edo in a grain bin and onto a ship. The ship had traveled only two days down the coast before pulling back into port and unceremoniously dumping Kai onto the shore. Apparently, that was as far as the favor to Razan would take him. He had been alone since then, but the Tokugawa were looking for him. He had run into the first squad of hunters while on the road and had been forced to defend himself. The second squad offered him all of their food, a tent, and a suit of armor. Apparently, Ienobu's message had made quite an impact even within the Tokugawa ranks. After that Kai decided to travel off the road and not test his luck a third time.

While he traveled, he thought over the events of the preceding year. He had lost so much, found more, and then lost it as well. The dream still came to him more nights than not, but it had changed after the events in Edo. The blood pouring out of Akemi's mouth soon became a giant wave. That wave crashed down on Ienobu, and Kai was forced to watch helplessly as the young man drowned.

Kai slept only fitfully that night and set off early the next

127

morning despite the chill in the air. He walked all day, pausing only briefly to eat. It was the last of his food. Gazing up at the sun, he reckoned it was early afternoon. He would need to find assistance and determine his location, and that meant getting back on the road. As he came closer, he heard a cart coming down the road. He hid behind a tree in a place to view the cart as it passed. When it came around the bend, Kai saw an older man driving a sway-backed horse. Kai moved out to the road, and when the man came close enough, Kai called to him, "Good sir, might I ask who is your lord?"

"My lord is called Mori Hidenari. You passed into his land when you crossed yonder ridge," the old man said pointing an arthritic finger at the mountain Kai had climbed the day before. With his location confirmed, Kai felt a weight fall off of him. He knew enough of the names of the lords in this area to put up a convincing front, and the Kikkawa mon on his back would lend credence.

"Might I ask you how far a journey Hagi might be?" Kai asked.

The old man thought for a while, "I would say Hagi lays another three days off to the south. If you are heading that way, it might be best to follow this road to the next village."

"You have done me two favors if I might beg a third, may I ride in your wagon for a while? I have been on the road for many days, and I am quite footsore," Kai asked. The old man motioned for Kai to climb up.

Kai clambered up to the cart and moved his hand down to keep his scabbard out of the way of his leg. The weight of the blade on his hip reassured him. His enemies had taken much from him, but he had managed to recover his soul.

A Timeline of Events

Actual Historic Events		Fictional Events
1600 AD	The Battle of Sekigahara	Kai's birth
1603	Ieyasu named Shogun	
1604	Iemitsu born	
1605	Ieyasu resigns	
	Hidetada becomes Shogun	
1606	Tokugawa Tadanaga born	
	Hotta Masamori born	
1607	Tokugawa Masako born	
1619		Ienobu born
1616	Ieyasu dies	
1620	Masako marries Emperor Mizunoo	
1623	Hidetada resigns	
	Iemitsu becomes Shogun	
1624	Future Empress Meisho	
	born to Masako and Mizunoo	
1629	Mizunoo retires	
	Meisho becomes empress	
1632	Hidetada dies	Story begins
1633	Hotta promoted by Iemitsu	Story ends
1634	Tadanaga commits seppuku	
	at Iemitsu's demand	
1635	Sankin-kotai mandated for	
	Tozama daimyo	
1637	Iemitsu's first child	
	Chiyohime born	
1642	Sankin-kotai mandated	
	for Fudai daimyo	

About The Author

Shane McInnis is a self-professed nerd with an overactive imagination. He spent his youth reading whatever he could put his hands on from the encyclopedia to the latest issue of X-Men. During college, his interests drew him deeper into the examination of the day to day lives of people in the past, and he holds a Master of Arts in History. Shane shares this passion with his college students, his wife, and anyone else courteous enough (to pretend) to listen. He has written scholarly non-fiction, graphic novels, short stories, and other works of fiction. Shane has traveled around the world visiting places from the cradles of civilization in the Near East to the capital cities of Europe. He calls the Pine Belt of South Mississippi home and works hard to break down the stereotypes of the region and those within it.

Made in the USA
Lexington, KY
07 November 2019

56700308R00085